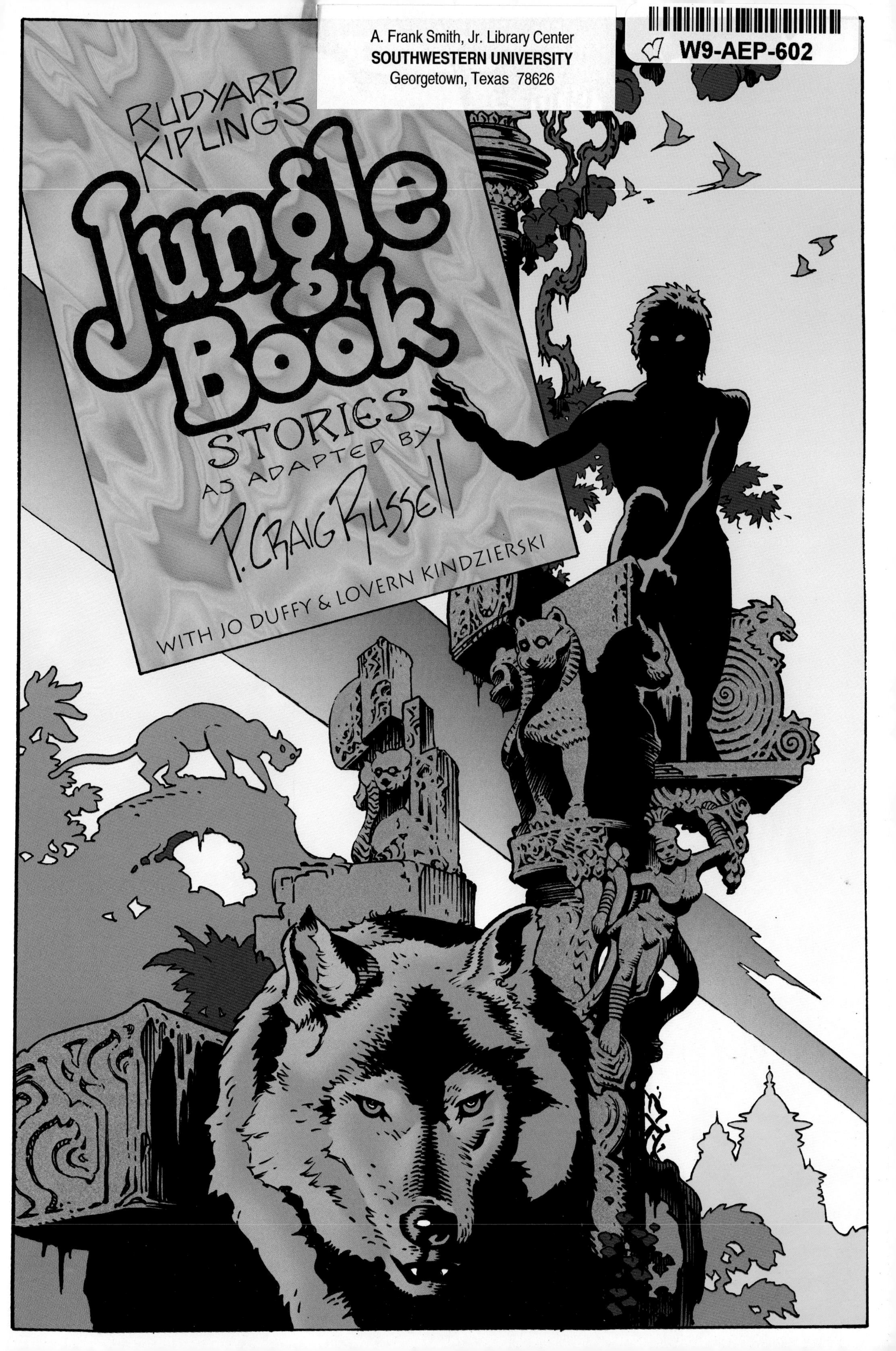

RUDYARD KIPLING'S
Jungle Book
STORIES
AS ADAPTED BY
P. CRAIG RUSSELL
WITH JO DUFFY & LOVERN KINDZIERSKI

Also available by Russell:
The Fairy Tales of Oscar Wilde
Vol.1: $15.95
Vol.2: $15.95
P&H: $3 1st item, $1 each addt'l.

We have over 150 graphic novels, write for
our complete color catalog:
NBM
185 Madison Ave. Ste 1504
New York, NY 10016
See our website: http://www.nbmpub.com

ISBN 1-56163-152-3

The King's Ankus script: Jo Duffy
The Spring Running coloring: Jessica
Kindzierski and Digital Chameleon.
Lettering by Bill Pearson.

Printed in Hong Kong

5 4 3 2 1

P. CRAIG RUSSELL 91·95

These are the four that are never content:
that have never been filled since the dews began--
Jacala's mouth, and the glut of the Kite,
and the hands of the ape,
and the eyes of Man. --JUNGLE SAYING
The King's Ankus
by Rudyard Kipling
OP. 19
ADAPTED FOR COMICS BY P. CRAIG RUSSELL

KAA, THE BIG ROCK PYTHON, HAD CHANGED HIS SKIN FOR PERHAPS THE TWO HUNDREDTH TIME SINCE HIS BIRTH...
...AND MOWGLI, THE MAN-CUB, WHO HAD BEEN RAISED BY THE WOLVES, AND WAS ACCEPTED NOW BY ALL AS THE MASTER OF THE JUNGLE...
...WENT TO CONGRATULATE HIM, FOR MOWGLI CARRIED HIS MANNERS AS HE CARRIED HIS KNIFE, AND THAT NEVER LEFT HIM.
GOOD HUNTING.

GOOD HUNTING, LITTLE BROTHER.
KAA VERY COURTEOUSLY PACKED HIMSELF SO THAT THE BOY WAS RESTING IN A LIVING ARMCHAIR, BESIDE WHERE THE OLD, BROKEN SKIN LAY.
EVEN TO THE SCALES OF THE EYES IT IS PERFECT.
STRANGE TO SEE THE COVERING OF ONE'S OWN HEAD AT ONE'S OWN FEET.
AYE, BUT I LACK FEET, AND SINCE THIS IS THE CUSTOM OF ALL MY PEOPLE, I DO NOT FIND IT STRANGE.
HOW LOOKS THE NEW COAT?

THE TURTLE IS HARDER BACKED, BUT NOT SO GAY. THE FROG IS MORE GAY, BUT NOT SO HARD. IT IS BEAUTIFUL TO SEE, LIKE THE MOTTLING IN THE MOUTH OF A LILY.
A NEW SKIN NEVER COMES TO FULL COLOR BEFORE THE FIRST BATH. LET US BATHE.
I WILL CARRY THEE.
THEN THEIR REGULAR EVENING GAME BEGAN...
heh heh heh
NOW! NOW! NOW! LOOK! I TOUCH THEE HERE, HERE, AND HERE!
ARE THY HANDS NUMB? HERE AGAIN!
THE GAME ALWAYS ENDED ONE WAY...
GOOD HUNTING...

IT IS VERY GOOD. I REMEMBER WHEN I VISITED WITH THE MAN PACK...
AT THIS HOUR THEY WOULD SHUT THEMSELVES UP IN TRAPS, AWAY FROM ALL THE CLEAN WINDS, AND LAY UPON HARD PIECES OF WOOD...
...AND DRAW FOUL CLOTHS OVER THEIR HEADS, AND MAKE EVIL SONGS THROUGH THEIR NOSES.
IT IS BETTER IN THE JUNGLE.

SO THE JUNGLE GIVES THEE ALL THAT THOU HAST EVER DESIRED, LITTLE BROTHER?
NOT ALL, ELSE THERE WOULD BE A NEW AND STRONG TIGER TO KILL ONCE A MOON, WITH MY OWN HANDS.

I HAVE WISHED FOR THE SUN DURING THE RAINS, AND THE RAINS DURING THE HEAT OF SUMMER.
WHEN I AM HUNGRY, I WISH I HAD KILLED A GOAT, AND WHEN I HAVE KILLED A GOAT, I WISH IT WERE A BUCK.

BUT THUS DO ALL OF US FEEL.
HAST THOU NO OTHER DESIRE?
WHAT MORE CAN I WISH? I HAVE THE JUNGLE AND THE FAVOR OF THE JUNGLE. IS THERE MORE BETWEEN SUNRISE AND SUNSET?
THE COBRA SAID--

WHAT COBRA? I GIVE THE POISON PEOPLE THEIR OWN PATH. THEY CARRY DEATH IN THE FORE TOOTH, AND THAT IS NOT GOOD.

THREE OR FOUR MOONS SINCE, I HUNTED IN THE COLD LAIRS-- WHERE ONCE I HELPED SAVE THEE FROM THE MONKEY PEOPLE--
AND THE ONE I HUNTED FLED SHRIEKING THROUGH THE WALL OF A HOUSE WHICH WAS BROKEN, AND RAN INTO THE GROUND.
UNDER EARTH?

I FOLLOWED, AND HAVING KILLED AND FED, I SLEPT. WHEN I WAKED, I WENT FORWARD.
I CAME UPON A COBRA WITH A WHITE HOOD, WHO SPOKE OF THINGS BEYOND MY KNOWLEDGE...
...AND SHOWED ME MANY THINGS I HAD NEVER BEFORE SEEN.

NEW GAME? WAS IT GOOD HUNTING?
IT WAS NO GAME, AND WOULD HAVE BROKEN ALL MY TEETH, BUT THE WHITE HOOD SPOKE AS ONE WHO KNEW MEN, AND SAID THAT A MAN WOULD GIVE THE HOT BREATH UNDER HIS RIBS FOR THE SIGHT OF THOSE THINGS.
WE WILL LOOK. I REMEMBER NOW THAT I WAS ONCE A MAN.
SLOWLY, LITTLE BROTHER, SLOWLY.
I SPOKE OF THEE, NAMING THEE AS A MAN, AND THE HOOD SAID, "IT IS LONG SINCE I HAVE SEEN A MAN."
THEN IT MUST BE NEW GAME. AND YET THE POISON PEOPLE ARE UNFRIENDLY FOLK, WHO DO NOT TELL US WHEN GAME IS AFOOT.
IT IS NOT GAME. IT IS-- IT IS-- I CANNOT SAY WHAT IT IS.
WE WILL GO THERE. I HAVE NEVER SEEN A WHITE HOOD, AND I WISH TO SEE THE OTHER THINGS. DID HE KILL THEM?
THEY ARE ALL DEAD THINGS. HE SAYS HE IS THE KEEPER OF THEM ALL
AH! AS THE WOLF STANDS ABOVE MEAT HE HAS TAKEN TO HIS OWN LAIR.
LET US GO.

THE TWO SET OFF FOR THE COLD LAIRS...

AND BEFORE THEY WENT UNDERGROUND, MOWGLI CALLED OUT THE MASTER WORDS IN THE SNAKE'S TONGUE:

WE BE OF ONE BLOOD, YE AND I!

A SAFE LAIR, BUT OVER-FAR TO VISIT DAILY. AND NOW WHAT DO WE SEE?

AM I NOTHING?

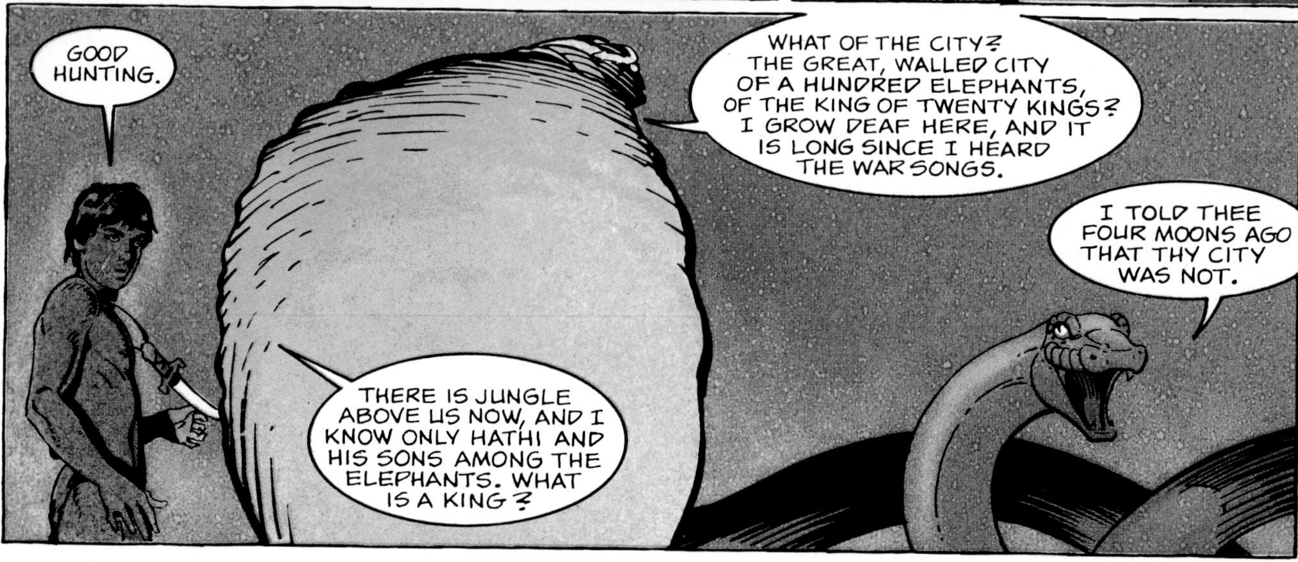
GOOD HUNTING.
WHAT OF THE CITY? THE GREAT, WALLED CITY OF A HUNDRED ELEPHANTS, OF THE KING OF TWENTY KINGS? I GROW DEAF HERE, AND IT IS LONG SINCE I HEARD THE WAR SONGS.
I TOLD THEE FOUR MOONS AGO THAT THY CITY WAS NOT.
THERE IS JUNGLE ABOVE US NOW, AND I KNOW ONLY HATHI AND HIS SONS AMONG THE ELEPHANTS. WHAT IS A KING?

THE GREAT CITY OF THE FOREST WHOSE GATES ARE GUARDED BY THE KING'S TOWERS CAN NEVER PASS. IT WAS BUILT BEFORE MY FATHER'S FATHER CAME FROM THE EGG...
...AND IT SHALL ENDURE WHEN MY SONS' SONS ARE AS WHITE AS I.
WHOSE CATTLE ARE YE?
IT IS A LOST TRAIL. I KNOW NOT HIS TALK.
NOR I. HE IS VERY OLD.
FATHER OF COBRAS, THERE IS ONLY THE JUNGLE HERE, AS THERE HAS BEEN FROM THE BEGINNING.
THEN WHO IS HE, UNAFRAID BEFORE ME, SPEAKING WITH A SNAKE'S TONGUE THROUGH A MAN'S LIPS?
MOWGLI, THEY CALL ME. THE WOLVES OF THE JUNGLE ARE MY PEOPLE AND KAA HERE IS MY BROTHER.
FATHER OF COBRAS, WHO ARE THOU?
I AM THE WARDEN OF THE KING'S TREASURE, PUT DOWN HERE BENEATH THE STONE TO TEACH DEATH TO THOSE WHO COME HERE TO STEAL.
MY MASTERS ARE THE BRAHMINS.
UMMM... I HAVE DEALT WITH ONE BRAHMIN ALREADY, IN THE MAN-PACK, AND...
EVIL COMES IN HERE, A LITTLE.

FIVE TIMES IN MY WARDSHIP HAS THE STONE BEEN LIFTED, ALWAYS TO PUT DOWN MORE TREASURE, AND NEVER TO TAKE AWAY--
IT IS THE TREASURE OF A HUNDRED KINGS.
BUT IT IS LONG SINCE THE STONE MOVED, AND I THINK MY CITY HAS FORGOTTEN.
THERE IS NO CITY. LOOK UP! YONDER ARE THE ROOTS OF GREAT TREES, TEARING THE STONES APART.
TWICE AND THRICE HAVE MEN FOUND THEIR WAY HERE, BUT THEY SPOKE NOT TILL I CAME ON THEM, AND THEY ONLY CRIED A LITTLE TIME.
BUT YE COME WITH LIES-- MAN AND SNAKE-- AND WOULD HAVE ME BELIEVE THAT MY CITY IS NOT, AND MY WARDSHIP IS ENDED.
LITTLE DO MEN CHANGE, BUT I CHANGE NEVER!
STOOP AND TAKE WHAT THOU WILT, MAN WITH THE SNAKE'S TONGUE.
IF THOU GOEST BACK ALIVE BY THE WAY THOU CAME, THE LESSER KINGS WILL BE THY SERVANTS.
AGAIN THE TRAIL IS LOST. HE IS SURELY MAD. FATHER OF COBRAS, I SEE NOTHING TO TAKE AWAY.
IT IS THE MADNESS OF DEATH UPON THE BOY! BEFORE THINE EYES CLOSE, I WILL ALLOW THEE THIS FAVOR.
LOOK THOU AND SEE WHAT MAN HAS NEVER SEEN BEFORE.
THEY DO NOT WELL IN THE JUNGLE WHO SPEAK TO MOWGLI OF FAVORS, BUT I WILL LOOK, IF THAT PLEASE THEE.

OHO! THIS IS LIKE THE STUFF THEY PLAY WITH IN THE MAN-PACK.

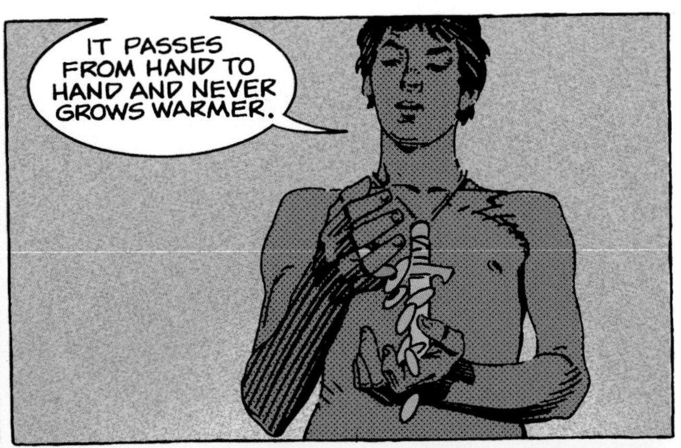
IT PASSES FROM HAND TO HAND AND NEVER GROWS WARMER.

KNIVES...!

BUT MY OWN HAS BETTER BALANCE.

?

THIS... HAS PICTURES ON IT, OF HATHI... OR OF SOME ELEPHANT.
IS IT NOT WORTH DYING TO BEHOLD? HAVE I NOT DONE THEE A GREAT FAVOR?
I DO NOT UNDERSTAND. THE THINGS ARE HARD AND COLD, AND BY NO MEANS GOOD TO EAT.
BUT THIS I DESIRE TO TAKE AWAY, THAT I MAY SEE IT IN THE SUN. THOU SAYEST THEY ARE ALL THINE?
WILT THOU GIVE IT TO ME, AND I WILL BRING THEE FROGS TO EAT!
THE ANKUS? ASSUREDLY, I WILL GIVE IT.
ALL THAT IS HERE I WILL GIVE THEE-- TILL THOU GOEST AWAY.

BUT I GO NOW. THIS PLACE IS COLD AND DARK, AND I WISH TO TAKE THE THORN-POINTED THING INTO THE JUNGLE.
LOOK BY THY FOOT. WHAT IS THERE?
IT IS THE BONE OF A MAN'S HEAD. AND THERE ARE TWO MORE.
THEY CAME TO TAKE THE TREASURE AWAY MANY YEARS AGO. I SPOKE TO THEM IN THE DARK, AND THEY LAY STILL.
BUT WHAT DO I NEED OF THIS TREASURE? IF THOU WILT GIVE ME THE ANKUS, IT IS GOOD HUNTING. IF THOU WILT NOT, IT IS GOOD HUNTING NONETHELESS.
I DO NOT FIGHT WITH THE POISON PEOPLE, AND I WAS TAUGHT THE MASTER WORD OF THY TRIBE.
THERE IS BUT ONE MASTER WORD HERE. IT IS MINE!

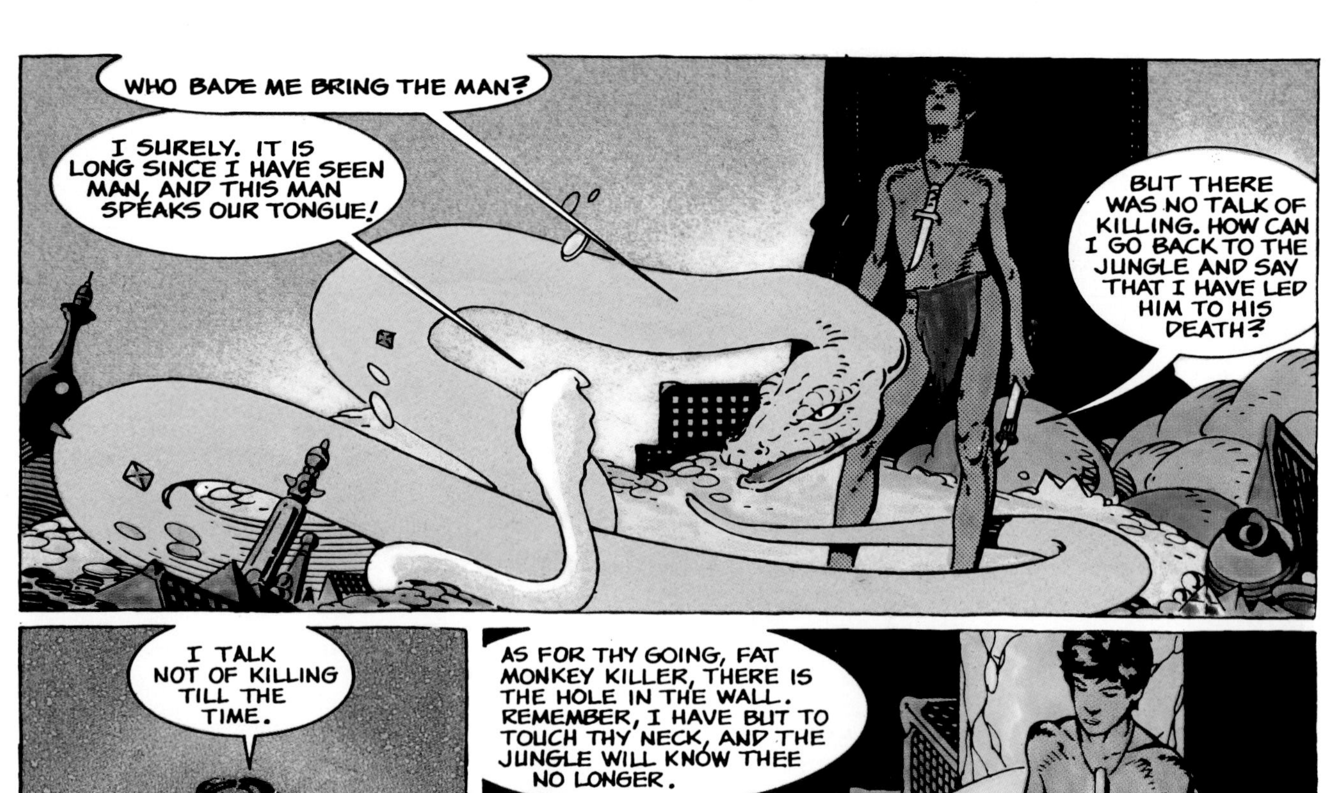
WHO BADE ME BRING THE MAN?
I SURELY. IT IS LONG SINCE I HAVE SEEN MAN, AND THIS MAN SPEAKS OUR TONGUE!
BUT THERE WAS NO TALK OF KILLING. HOW CAN I GO BACK TO THE JUNGLE AND SAY THAT I HAVE LED HIM TO HIS DEATH?

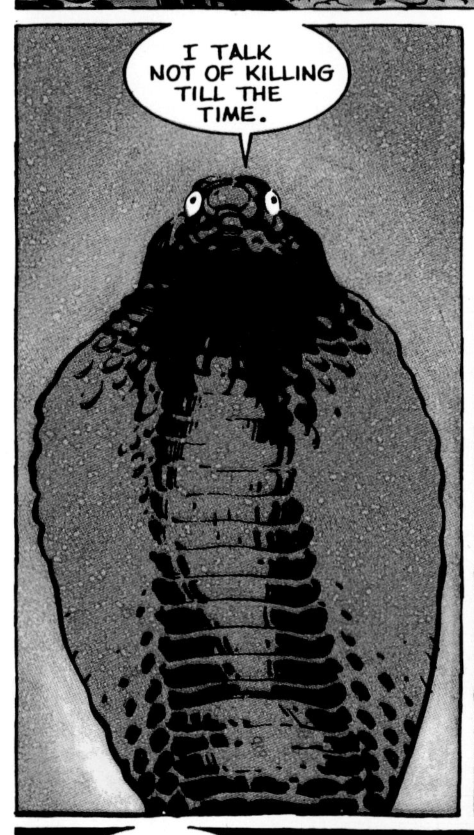
I TALK NOT OF KILLING TILL THE TIME.

AS FOR THY GOING, FAT MONKEY KILLER, THERE IS THE HOLE IN THE WALL. REMEMBER, I HAVE BUT TO TOUCH THY NECK, AND THE JUNGLE WILL KNOW THEE NO LONGER.
NEVER MAN CAME HERE THAT WENT AWAY WITH THE BREATH UNDER HIS RIBS. I AM THE WARDEN OF THE KING'S TREASURE.
BUT THOU, WHITE WORM OF THE DARK, I TELL THEE THERE IS NEITHER KING NOR CITY. THE JUNGLE IS ALL ABOUT US!

THERE IS STILL THE TREASURE!
WAIT A WHILE, KAA OF THE ROCKS, AND SEE THE BOY RUN. THERE IS ROOM FOR GREAT SPORT HERE. LIFE IS GOOD.

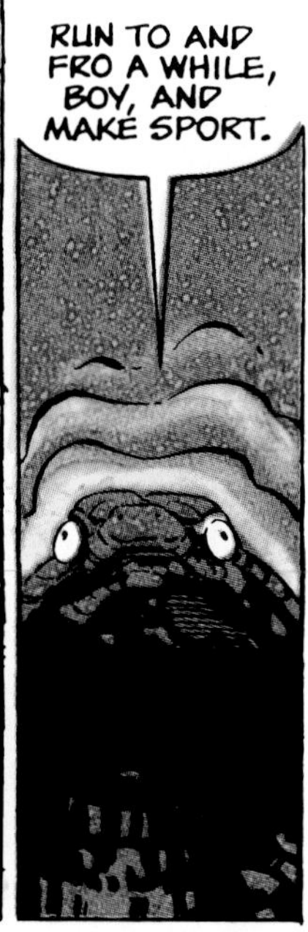
RUN TO AND FRO A WHILE, BOY, AND MAKE SPORT.

THE WHITE THING HAS DEALT WITH MEN OF THE MAN-PACK UNTIL NOW. HE DOES NOT KNOW ME.
HE HAS ASKED FOR THIS HUNTING.
LET HIM HAVE IT!
KILL!!
NO... NEVER, SAVE FOR FOOD. BUT LOOK YOU, KAA.
IT IS THUU-- THE POISON IS OLD AND DRIED UP, LIKE A ROTTED TREE STUMP.
THE KING'S TREASURE NEEDS A NEW WARDEN.
YOU RUN TO AND FRO TO MAKE SPORT, THUU!

I AM SHAMED! KILL ME!
THERE HAS BEEN TOO MUCH TALK OF KILLING.
WE WILL GO NOW.
I WILL TAKE THE THORN-POINTED THING, THUU, BECAUSE I HAVE WORSTED THEE.
SEE THEN THAT IT DOES NOT KILL THEE AT LAST. THERE IS ENOUGH IN THAT THING TO KILL ALL THE MEN OF MY CITY.
NOT LONG WILT THOU HOLD IT, JUNGLE MAN, NOR HE WHO TAKES IT FROM THEE! THEY WILL KILL AND KILL AND KILL FOR ITS SAKE.
I AM DRIED UP, BUT THE ANKUS WILL DO MY WORK.
IT IS DEATH!
IT IS DEATH!
IT IS DEATH
IN THE LIGHT, THE COLORED STONES ARE BRIGHTER EVEN THAN THE EYES OF BAGHEERA THE PANTHER. HE MUST SEE IT!
BUT WHAT DID THE THUU MEAN WHEN HE TALKED OF DEATH?
I CANNOT SAY. I AM SORROWFUL TO MY TAIL'S TAIL THAT HE FELT NOT THY KNIFE. THERE IS ALWAYS EVIL AT THE COLD LAIRS. ABOVEGROUND AND BELOW.
BUT NOW I AM HUNGRY. DOST THOU HUNT WITH ME THIS DAWN?
NO. BAGHEERA MUST SEE THIS THING.
GOOD HUNTING.
GOOD HUNTING.

MOWGLI DANCED OFF, FLOURISHING THE ANKUS, TILL HE CAME TO THAT PART OF THE JUNGLE BAGHEERA CHIEFLY USED, AND TOLD THE PANTHER ALL HIS ADVENTURES FROM BEGINNING TO END. WHEN HE CAME TO THE COBRA'S LAST WORDS, BAGHEERA PURRED APPROVINGLY.
THEN THE WHITE HOOD SPOKE THE THING THAT IS?
I WAS BORN IN THE KING'S CAGES, AND IT IS IN MY STOMACH THAT I KNOW SOME LITTLE OF MAN.
MANY MEN WOULD KILL THRICE IN A NIGHT FOR THE SAKE OF THAT LITTLE RED STONE ALONE.
BUT THE STONE MAKES IT HEAVY TO THE HAND.
MY LITTLE BRIGHT KNIFE IS BETTER, AND--SEE!
THE RED STONE IS NOT GOOD TO EAT. THEN, WHY WOULD THEY KILL?
MOWGLI, GO THOU TO SLEEP. THOU HAST LIVED AMONG MEN, AND--!
I REMEMBER. MEN KILL WHEN THEY ARE NOT HUNTING, FOR IDLENESS AND PLEASURE.
BAGHEERA, WAKE AGAIN. FOR WHAT USE WAS THIS THORN-POINTED THING MADE?
TO TEACH MAN'S LAW TO ELEPHANTS. HAVING NEITHER TEETH NOR CLAW, MEN MADE THIS TO THRUST INTO THE HEADS OF ELEPHANTS AND MAKE THE BLOOD FLOW.
THAT THING HAS TASTED THE BLOOD OF MANY SUCH AS HATHI.
ALWAYS MORE BLOOD WHEN I COME NEAR EVEN TO THE THINGS THE MAN PACK HAVE MADE.
IF I HAD KNOWN THIS, I WOULD NOT HAVE TAKEN IT.
I WILL USE IT NO MORE. LOOK!

SO MY HANDS ARE CLEAN OF DEATH.
THE THUU SAID DEATH WOULD FOLLOW ME.
HE IS OLD AND WHITE
AND MAD.
WHITE OR BLACK, OR DEATH OR LIFE, I AM GOING TO SLEEP, LITTLE BROTHER.
I CANNOT HUNT ALL NIGHT AND HOWL ALL DAY, AS DO SOME FOLK.
EEEEEE

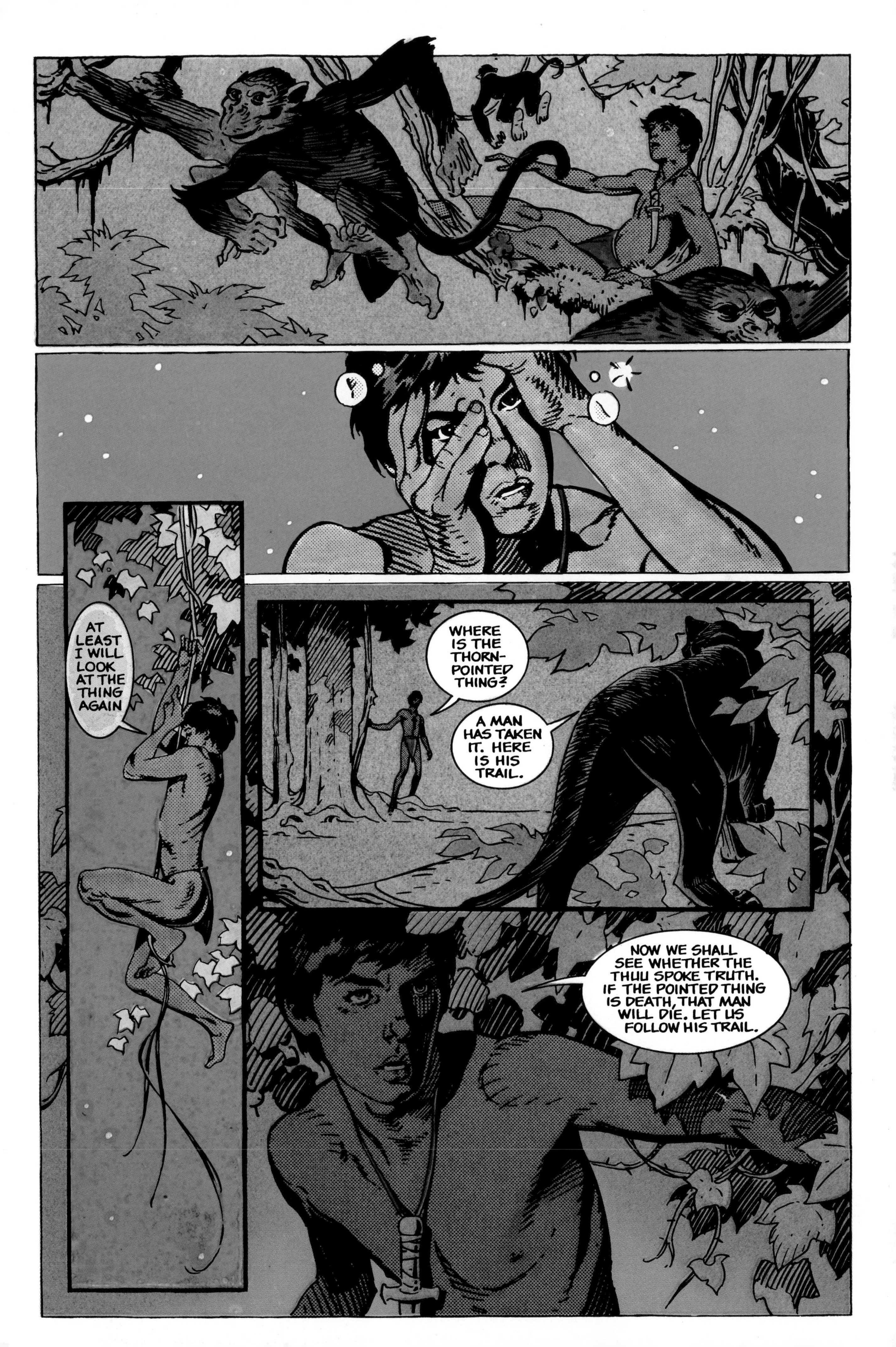
AT LEAST I WILL LOOK AT THE THING AGAIN
WHERE IS THE THORN-POINTED THING?
A MAN HAS TAKEN IT. HERE IS HIS TRAIL.
NOW WE SHALL SEE WHETHER THE THUU SPOKE TRUTH. IF THE POINTED THING IS DEATH, THAT MAN WILL DIE. LET US FOLLOW HIS TRAIL.

THINK YOU THE THORN-POINTED THING WILL TURN IN THE MAN'S HAND AND KILL HIM? THE THUU SAID IT WAS DEATH.
WE SHALL SEE WHEN WE FIND HIM. IT IS SINGLE FOOT-- THE MAN TRAVELS ALONE--AND THE WEIGHT OF THE THING HAS PRESSED HIS HEEL FAR INTO THE GROUND.
NOW HE RUNS SWIFTLY...
BUT WHY DOES HE TURN ASIDE HERE?
WAIT
HERE COMES ANOTHER TRAIL TO MEET HIM. THE SECOND TRAIL IS A SMALLER FOOT, AND THE TOES TURN INWARD.
IT IS A GOND HUNTER. SEE, HERE IS WHERE HE DRAGGED HIS BOW ON THE GRASS. THE TRAIL TURNED ASIDE, BECAUSE BIG FOOT HID FROM LITTLE FOOT!
THAT IS TRUE. NOW, LET US EACH TAKE ONE TRAIL, AND CRY IT TO EACH OTHER.
I AM BIG FOOT, THOU ART LITTLE FOOT.
I, BIG FOOT, TURN ASIDE HERE. NOW I HIDE ME BEHIND THE ROCK AND STAND STILL, NOT DARING TO SHIFT MY FEET.
NOW I, LITTLE FOOT, COME TO THE ROCK, AND SIT AND WAIT UNDER IT, FOR THE MARK OF MY FEET IS DEEP HERE.
I ALSO. I REST THE THORN-POINTED THING UPON A STONE. IT SLIPS, FOR HERE IS THE SCRATCH IT LEFT...

BROKEN BRANCHES HERE... AH, IT IS PLAIN NOW. I WANT BIG FOOT TO HEAR ME!
I GO FAR AWAY
TO WHERE THE NOISE OF FALLING WATER
WILL COVER
MY NOISE
AND I
WAIT
I COME FROM BEHIND THE ROCK ON MY KNEES, DRAGGING THE THORN-POINTED THING. SEEING NO ONE, I RUN.
WHERE ARE THOU, LITTLE FOOT... LITTLE BROTHER?
HERE!
UM! THE TWO RUN SIDE BY SIDE, DRAWING NEARER...
THEY HAVE MET. GOOD HUNTING-- LOOK! HERE STOOD LITTLE FOOT, WITH HIS KNEE ON A ROCK, AND YONDER IS BIG FOOT!
WAS THE THUU SO OLD AND MAD, LITTLE BROTHER? HERE IS ONE DEATH AT LEAST.

FOLLOW ON, BUT WHERE IS THE DRINKER OF ELEPHANT'S BLOOD-- THE RED-EYED THORN?
LITTLE FOOT HAS IT, PERHAPS. IT IS SINGLE FOOT AGAIN, NOW.
AGAIN
THAT WAS DONE WITH A BAMBOO. THE FATHER OF COBRAS-- I AM SORRY THAT I MADE JEST OF HIM--KNEW THE BREED OF MAN WELL. SAID I NOT THAT MEN KILL FOR IDLENESS?
INDEED, THEY KILLED FOR THE SAKE OF THE RED AND BLUE STONES. REMEMBER, I WAS IN THE KING'S CAGES.
ONE, TWO, THREE, FOUR TRACKS OF MEN WITH SHOD FEET. WHAT EVIL HAD THE LITTLE GOND DONE TO THEM?
SEE, THEY TALKED TOGETHER, ALL FIVE, STANDING UP, BEFORE THEY KILLED HIM.

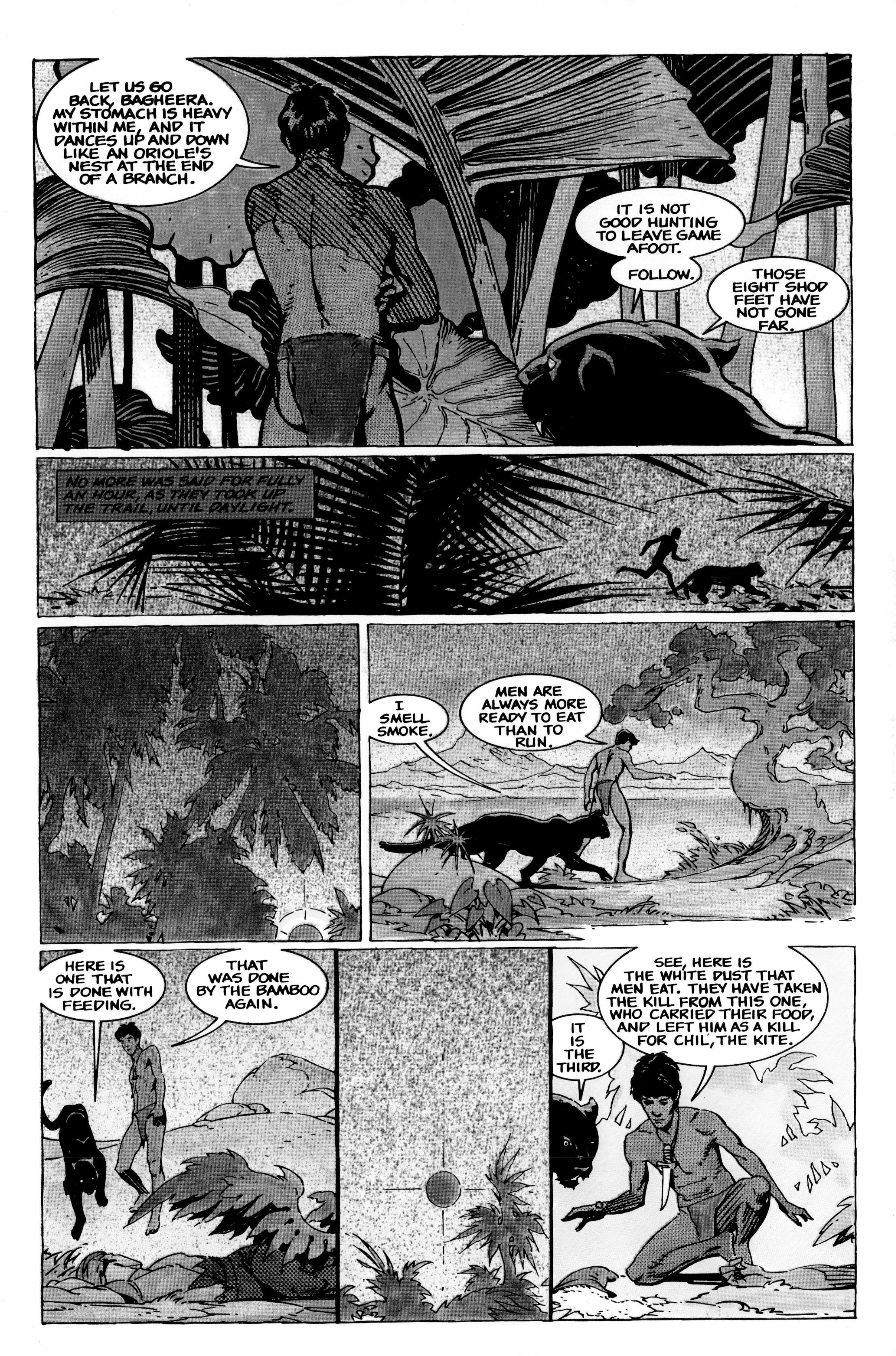
LET US GO BACK, BAGHEERA. MY STOMACH IS HEAVY WITHIN ME, AND IT DANCES UP AND DOWN LIKE AN ORIOLE'S NEST AT THE END OF A BRANCH.
IT IS NOT GOOD HUNTING TO LEAVE GAME AFOOT.
FOLLOW.
THOSE EIGHT SHOD FEET HAVE NOT GONE FAR.
NO MORE WAS SAID FOR FULLY AN HOUR, AS THEY TOOK UP THE TRAIL, UNTIL DAYLIGHT.
I SMELL SMOKE.
MEN ARE ALWAYS MORE READY TO EAT THAN TO RUN.
HERE IS ONE THAT IS DONE WITH FEEDING.
THAT WAS DONE BY THE BAMBOO AGAIN.
IT IS THE THIRD.
SEE, HERE IS THE WHITE DUST THAT MEN EAT. THEY HAVE TAKEN THE KILL FROM THIS ONE, WHO CARRIED THEIR FOOD, AND LEFT HIM AS A KILL FOR CHIL, THE KITE.

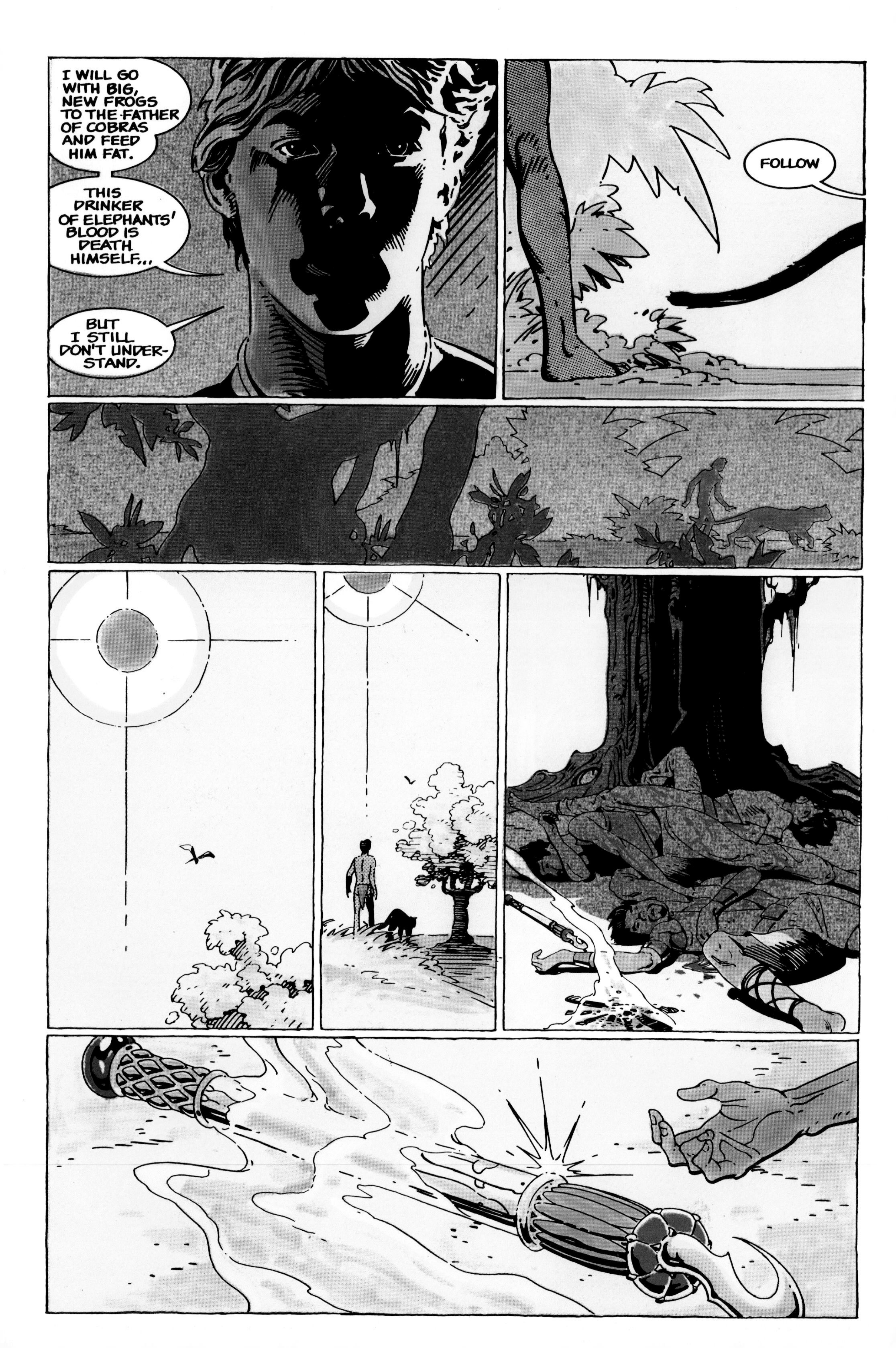
I WILL GO WITH BIG, NEW FROGS TO THE FATHER OF COBRAS AND FEED HIM FAT.
THIS DRINKER OF ELEPHANTS' BLOOD IS DEATH HIMSELF...
BUT I STILL DON'T UNDERSTAND.
FOLLOW

THE THING WORKS QUICKLY; ALL ENDS HERE. HOW DID *THESE* DIE, MOWGLI? THERE IS NO MARK ON ANY.
PTOO
APPLE OF DEATH! THE FIRST MUST HAVE MADE IT READY IN THE FOOD FOR *THESE*, WHO KILLED HIM, HAVING FIRST KILLED THE GOND.
GOOD HUNTING *INDEED*. WHAT NOW? MUST THOU AND I KILL EACH OTHER FOR YONDER RED-EYED SLAYER?
BETWEEN US TWO IT CAN DO NO WRONG, FOR WE DO NOT DESIRE WHAT MEN DESIRE. IF IT BE LEFT HERE, IT WILL ASSUREDLY CONTINUE TO KILL MEN ONE AFTER ANOTHER.
I HAVE NO LOVE TO MEN, BUT EVEN I WOULD NOT HAVE THEM DIE SIX IN A NIGHT.
WHAT MATTER? THEY ARE ONLY MEN. THEY KILLED ONE ANOTHER, AND WERE WELL PLEASED, THAT FIRST LITTLE WOODSMAN HUNTED WELL.
THEY ARE CUBS NONE THE LESS; AND A CUB WILL DROWN HIMSELF TO BITE THE MOONLIGHT ON THE WATER.
THE FAULT WAS MINE.
I WILL NEVER AGAIN BRING INTO THE JUNGLE STRANGE THINGS — NOT THOUGH THEY BE AS BEAUTIFUL AS FLOWERS.
THIS — GOES BACK TO THE FATHER OF THE COBRAS.
BUT FIRST WE MUST SLEEP.

TWO NIGHTS LATER, AS THE WHITE COBRA SAT MOURNING IN THE DARKNESS OF THE VAULT., ASHAMED, AND ROBBED, AND ALONE . . .

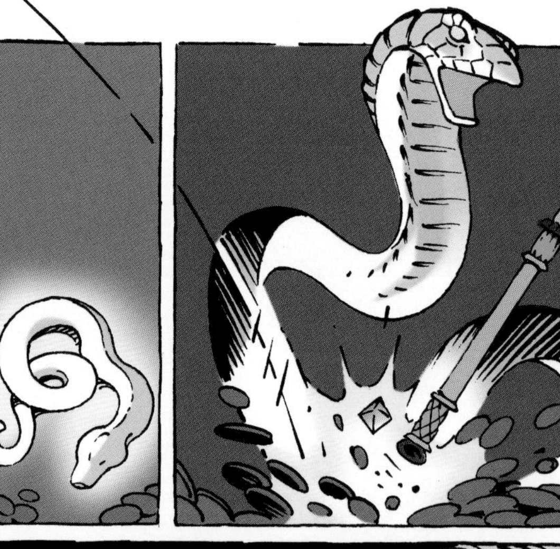

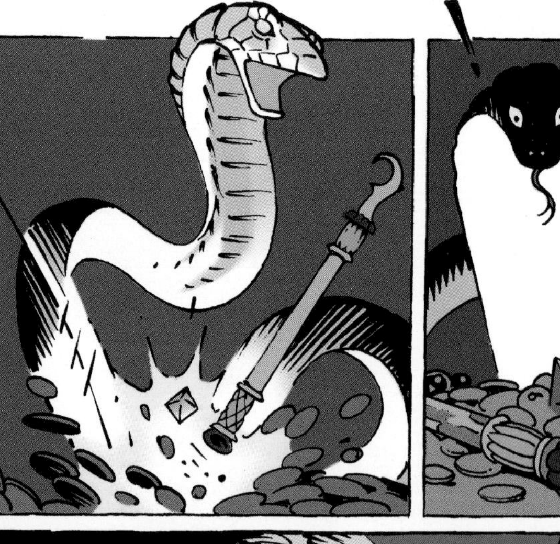

FATHER OF COBRAS, GET THEE A YOUNG AND RIPE ONE OF THINE OWN PEOPLE TO HELP THEE GUARD THE KING'S TREASURE, SO THAT NO MAN MAY COME AWAY ALIVE ANY MORE.

AH-HA! IT RETURNS, THEN. I *SAID* THE THING WAS DEATH. HOW COMES IT THAT THOU ART STILL ALIVE?
BY THE BULL THAT BROUGHT ME, I DO NOT KNOW.
THAT THING HAS KILLED SIX TIMES IN A NIGHT.
LET HIM GO OUT NO MORE.
·END·

EPILOGUE
Ere Mor the peacock flutters, ere the Monkey people cry,
Ere Chil the Kite swoops down a furlong sheer,
Through the jungle very softly flits a shadow and a sigh--
He is fear, O little hunter, he is fear!

Very softly down the glade runs a waiting, watching shade,
And the whisper spreads and widens far and near:
And the sweat is on thy brow,
For he passes even now--
He is fear, O little brother, he is fear.

Rudyard Kipling's
Red Dog
op. 25
1987
Adapted for Comics by P. Craig Russell
THESE WERE MY COMPANIONS GOING FORTH BY NIGHT
(CHIL! LOOK YOU FOR CHIL!)
NOW COME I TO WHISTLE THEM THE ENDING OF THE FIGHT.
(CHIL! VANGUARDS OF CHIL!)
TATTERED FLANK AND SUNKEN EYE, OPEN MOUTH AND RED,
LOCKED AND LANK AND LONE THEY LIE, THE DEAD UPON THE DEAD.
HERE'S AN END OF EVERY TRAIL—
...AND HERE MY HOSTS ARE FED.
BUT WE MUST BEGIN EACH STORY AT THE BEGINNING...
FATHER AND MOTHER WOLF DIED, AND MOWGLI CRIED THE DEATH SONG OVER THEM.
BALOO GREW VERY OLD AND STIFF, AND EVEN BAGHEERA, WHOSE NERVES WERE STEEL AND WHOSE MUSCLES WERE IRON, SEEMED SLOWER AT THE KILL, AND AKELA TURNED GRAY TO MILKY WHITE WITH PURE AGE. BUT THE YOUNG WOLVES THROVE AND INCREASED, AND AKELA TOLD THEM THAT THEY OUGHT TO GATHER THEMSELVES TOGETHER AND FOLLOW THE LAW, AND RUN UNDER ONE HEAD, AS BEFITTED THE FREE PEOPLE.
THOSE WERE THE DAYS OF GOOD HUNTING. NO STRANGER DARED TO BREAK INTO THE JUNGLES THAT BELONGED TO MOWGLI'S PEOPLE, AND THE YOUNG WOLVES GREW FAT AND STRONG.
ONE TWILIGHT, WHEN HE WAS TROTTING LEISURELY ACROSS THE RANGES...

LETTERING · BILL PEARSON

IT IS WHAT THEY CALL IN THE JUNGLE THE **PHEEAL**, A KIND OF SHRIEK THAT THE JACKEL GIVES WHEN HE IS HUNTING BEHIND A TIGER, OR WHEN THERE IS SOME BIG KILLING AFOOT.
THERE IS NO STRIPED ONE WOULD DARE KILL HERE.
THAT IS NOT THE CRY OF THE FORERUNNER. IT IS SOME GREAT KILLING. LISTEN!

AAARRROOOOOOOOOO.......

DHOLE
DHOLE
DHOLE
DHOLE...

GOOD HUNTING? UNDER WHOSE HEADSHIP ARE THEE?
GOOD HUNTING! UNDER NO HEADSHIP. WON-TOLLA AM I- A SOLITARY WOLF.
WHAT MOVES?
THE DHOLES, THE DHOLES OF THE DEKKAN-- RED DOG THE KILLER! RED HUNTERS, ALL-GROWN DOGS OF THEIR PACK, HEAVY AND STRONG. THEY CAME NORTH FROM THE SOUTH, SAYING THE DEKKAN WAS EMPTY AND KILLING OUT BY THE WAY. WHEN THIS MOON WAS NEW THERE WERE FOUR TO ME-- MY MATE AND THREE CUBS.
AT MIDNIGHT I HEARD THEM TOGETHER, FULL TONGUE ON THE TRAIL. AT THE DAWN-WIND I FOUND THEM STIFF IN THE GRASS.
THEN SOUGHT I MY BLOOD RIGHT AND FOUND THE DHOLE.
HOW MANY?
I DO NOT KNOW. THREE OF THEM WILL KILL NO MORE, BUT AT THE LAST THEY DROVE ME LIKE THE BUCK, ON THREE LEGS THEY DROVE ME.
GIVE ME A LITTLE STRENGTH, FREE PEOPLE, AND I ALSO WILL KILL! MY LAIR IS EMPTY THAT WAS FULL WHEN THIS MOON WAS NEW, AND THE BLOOD DEBT IS NOT ALL PAID.

IT IS BETTER TO DIE IN THE FULL PACK THAN LEADERLESS AND ALONE.
AKELA!
IT IS GOOD HUNTING, AND-- MY LAST. BUT AS MEN LIVE, THOU HAST VERY MANY MORE NIGHTS AND DAYS, LITTLE BROTHER.
GO NORTH AND LIE DOWN, AND IF ANY WOLF LIVE AFTER THE DHOLE HAS GONE BY, HE SHALL BRING THEE WORD OF THE FIGHT.
AH! MUST I GO TO THE MARSHES AND CATCH LITTLE FISH AND SLEEP IN A TREE, OR MUST I ASK HELP OF THE BANDAR-LOG AND EAT NUTS WHILE THE PACK FIGHTS BELOW?
IT IS TO THE DEATH! THOU HAST NEVER MET THE DHOLES-- THE RED KILLERS. HATHI THE ELEPHANT MOVES ASIDE FROM THEIR LINE, AND UNTIL THEY ARE ALL KILLED, OR TILL GAME IS SCARCE, THEY GO FORWARD, KILLING AS THEY GO. EVEN THE STRIPED ONE...
AOWA! LISTEN NOW: THERE WAS A WOLF, MY FATHER, AND THERE WAS A WOLF, MY MOTHER. AND THERE WAS AN OLD GREY WOLF (NOT TOO WISE: HE IS WHITE NOW) WAS MY FATHER AND MOTHER. THEREFORE...
I SAY THAT WHEN THE DHOLES COME, MOWGLI AND THE FREE PEOPLE ARE OF ONE SKIN FOR THAT HUNTING. I SAY THAT THIS MY KNIFE SHALL BE AS A TOOTH TO THE PACK.
THIS IS MY WORD WHICH HAS GONE FROM ME.
THOU DOST NOT KNOW THE DHOLE, MAN WITH A WOLF'S TONGUE.

BUT FOR YE, FREE PEOPLE, MY COUNSEL IS THAT YE GO NORTH TILL THE DHOLE ARE GONE.
HEAR THE OUTLIER! WE MUST GO NORTH LEST BY ANY CHANCE WE MEET THE DHOLE. HE MUST KILL OUT OUR HUNTING-GROUNDS WHILE WE LIE HID IN THE NORTH TILL IT PLEASE HIM TO GIVE US OUR OWN AGAIN.
HE IS A DOG-- AND THE PUP OF A DOG-- RED, YELLOW-BELLIED, LAIRLESS, AND HAIRED BETWEEN EVERY TOE!
SURELY WE MUST RUN AWAY, AND BEG LEAVE OF THE PEOPLES OF THE NORTH FOR THE OFFAL OF DEAD CATTLE.
YE KNOW THE SAYING: 'NORTH ARE THE VERMIN; SOUTH ARE THE LICE. WE ARE THE JUNGLE.'
CHOOSE YE, O CHOOSE. IT IS GOOD HUNTING! FOR THE PACK-- FOR THE FULL PACK-- FOR THE LAIR AND THE LETTER; FOR THE IN-KILL AND THE OUT-KILL; FOR THE MATE THAT DRIVES THE DOE AND THE LITTLE CUB WITHIN THE CAVE...
IT IS MET!
IT IS MET!
IT IS MET!!

BAARRROOOOOOOOO!
STAY WITH THESE, PHAO AND AKELA. I GO TO COUNT THE DOGS; WE SHALL NEED EVERY TOOTH.
IT IS DEATH! WHAT CAN SUCH A HAIRLESS ONE DO AGAINST THE RED DOG...
THOU ART INDEED AN OUTLIER, BUT WE WILL SPEAK WHEN THE DHOLES ARE DEAD.
GOOD HUNTING, ALL!

WHOOF!!
KSSHA!
IS THIS JUNGLE WORK, TO STAMP AND RAMP AND UNDO A NIGHT'S HUNTING?..
THE FAULT WAS MINE. INDEED, I WAS SEEKING THEE, FLATHEAD. THERE IS NONE LIKE THEE IN THE JUNGLE, WISE, OLD, STRONG, AND MOST BEAUTIFUL KAA.
NOW WHITHER DOES THIS TRAIL LEAD? NOT A MOON SINCE THERE WAS A MANLING WITH A KNIFE THREW STONES AT MY HEAD AND CALLED ME BAD LITTLE TREE-CAT NAMES.

NOW THIS SAME MANLING COMES WITH SOFT, TICKLING WORDS TO THIS SAME FLAT-HEAD, TELLING HIM THAT HE IS WISE, AND STRONG, AND BEAUTIFUL, AND THIS SAME OLD FLATHEAD BELIEVES AND COILS A PLACE, THUS, FOR THIS SAME STONE-THROWING MAN-LING, AND...
...ART THEE AT EASE NOW? COULD BAGHEERA GIVE THEE SO GOOD A RESTING-PLACE?
THE BOY REACHED OUT IN THE DARKNESS AND GATHERED IN THE SUPPLE, CABLE-LIKE NECK TILL KAA'S HEAD RESTED ON HIS SHOULDER, AND THEN HE TOLD HIM ALL THAT HAD HAPPENED IN THE JUNGLE THAT NIGHT.
WISE I MAY BE, BUT DEAF I SURELY AM. I HEARD NOTHING.
I HAVE NOT SEEN YET, BUT, OH, KAA, IT WILL BE GOOD HUNTING! FEW OF US WILL SEE ANOTHER MOON.
BUT WHAT IS IN THY STOMACH TO DO WHEN THE DHOLE COME?
THEY MUST SWIM THE WAINGANGA. I THOUGHT TO MEET THEM WITH MY KNIFE IN THE SHALLOWS, THE PACK BEHIND ME, AND SO STABBING AND THRUSTING WE MIGHT TURN THEM DOWNSTREAM, OR COOL THEIR THROATS A LITTLE.
THE DHOLE DO NOT TURN AND THEIR THROATS ARE HOT.
HAST THOU A BETTER PLAN, KAA?
I HAVE SEEN A HUNDRED AND A HUNDRED RAINS. WHAT IS-HAS BEEN. WHAT WILL BE IS NO MORE THAN A FORGOTTEN YEAR STRIKING BACKWARDS. BE STILL WHILE I COUNT THOSE MY YEARS.

ZZZZZ

KKKKKKSSSSSSSSSSSHHHH
I HAVE SEEN ALL THE DEAD SEASONS AND THE GREAT TREES AND THE OLD ELEPHANTS AND THE ROCKS THAT WERE BARE AND SHARP-POINTED ERE THE MOSS GREW. ART THOU STILL ALIVE, MANLING?
YAWWNN... IT IS ONLY A LITTLE AFTER MOON RISE. I DO NOT UNDERSTAND...
HSSH! I AM AGAIN KAA. NOW WE WILL GO TO THE RIVER, AND I WILL SHOW THEE WHAT IS TO BE DONE AGAINST THE DHOLE.

THE SPLIT AND WEATHER-WORN ROCKS OF THE GORGE OF THE WAINGANGA HAD BEEN USED SINCE THE BEGINNING OF THE JUNGLE BY THE LITTLE PEOPLE OF THE ROCKS--THE BUSY, FURIOUS, BLACK, WILD BEES OF INDIA. FOR CENTURIES THE LITTLE PEOPLE HAD HIVED AND SWARMED FROM CLEFT TO CLEFT, STAINING THE WHITE MARBLE WITH STALE HONEY, AND MADE THEIR COMBS TALL AND DEEP AND BLACK IN THE DARK OF THE INNER CAVES, AND NEITHER MAN NOR BEAST NOR FIRE NOR WATER HAD EVER TOUCHED THEM.
AS MOWGLI LISTENED, HE HEARD MORE THAN ONCE THE RUSTLE AND SLIDE OF A HONEY-LOADED COMB TURNING OVER OR FALLING AWAY SOMEWHERE IN THE DARK GALLERIES. THEN A BOOMING OF ANGRY WINGS AND THE SULLEN DRIP...DRIP...DRIP...
THIS IS THE PLACE OF DEATH. WHY DO WE COME HERE?

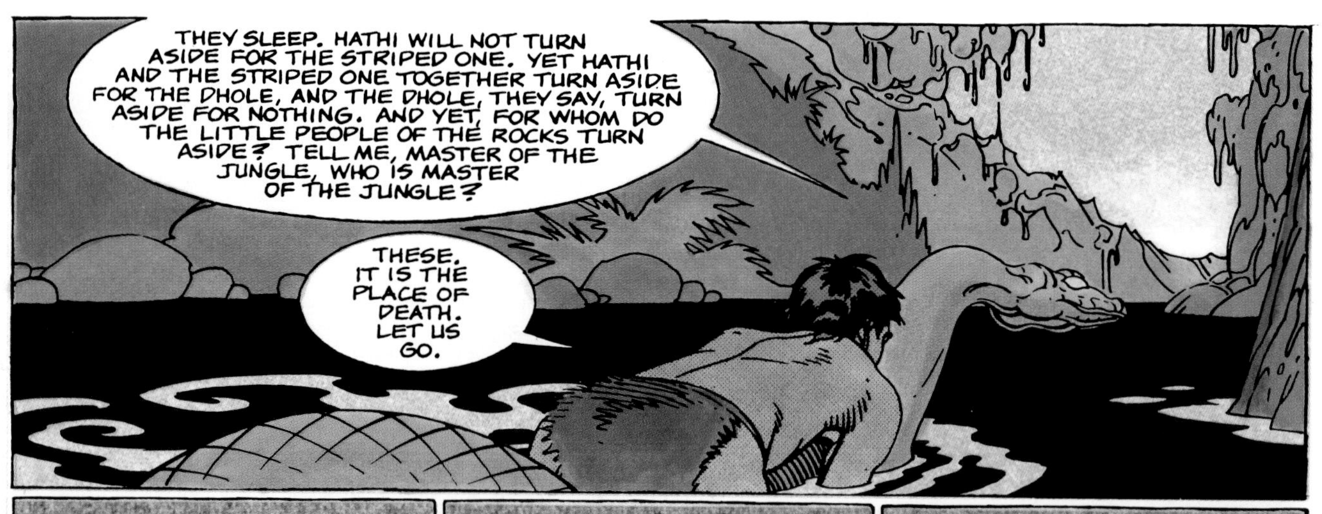
THEY SLEEP. HATHI WILL NOT TURN ASIDE FOR THE STRIPED ONE. YET HATHI AND THE STRIPED ONE TOGETHER TURN ASIDE FOR THE DHOLE, AND THE DHOLE, THEY SAY, TURN ASIDE FOR NOTHING. AND YET, FOR WHOM DO THE LITTLE PEOPLE OF THE ROCKS TURN ASIDE? TELL ME, MASTER OF THE JUNGLE, WHO IS MASTER OF THE JUNGLE?
THESE. IT IS THE PLACE OF DEATH. LET US GO.

THEY DO NOT WAKE TILL THE DAWN. NOW I WILL TELL THEE. A HUNTED BUCK FROM THE SOUTH, MANY, MANY RAINS AGO, CAME HITHER FROM THE SOUTH, NOT KNOWING THE JUNGLE, A PACK ON HIS TRAIL. BEING MADE BLIND BY FEAR, HE LEAPED FROM ABOVE...

THE SUN WAS HIGH, AND THE LITTLE PEOPLE WERE MANY, AND VERY ANGRY. MANY, TOO, WERE THOSE OF THE PACK WHO LEAPED INTO THE WAINGANGA, BUT THEY WERE DEAD ERE THEY TOOK WATER.

THOSE WHO DID NOT LEAP DIED ALSO IN THE ROCKS ABOVE. BUT THE BUCK LIVED.
HOW?
BECAUSE HE CAME FIRST, RUNNING FOR HIS LIFE, LEAPING ERE THE LITTLE PEOPLE WERE AWARE, AND WAS IN THE RIVER WHEN THEY GATHERED TO KILL.

THE PACK, FOLLOWING, WAS ALTOGETHER LOST UNDER THE WEIGHT OF THE LITTLE PEOPLE, WHO HAD BEEN ROUSED BY THE FEET OF THAT BUCK.

?!

THE BUCK LIVED?

AT LEAST HE DID NOT DIE *THEN!*

HE DID NOT DIE THEN, THOUGH NONE WAITED HIS COMING DOWN WITH A STRONG BODY TO HOLD HIM SAFE AGAINST THE WATER, AS A CERTAIN OLD, FAT, DEAF, YELLOW FLATHEAD WOULD WAIT FOR A MANLING.
WHAT IS IN THY STOMACH?
IT IS TO PULL THE VERY WHISKERS OF DEATH.
LOOK NOW, IF THE DHOLE FOLLOW THEE--
AS SURELY THEY WILL. HO! HO! I HAVE MANY LITTLE THORNS UNDER MY TONGUE TO PRICK INTO THEIR HIDES.
IF THEY FOLLOW THEE HOT AND BLIND, LOOKING ONLY AT THY SHOULDERS, THOSE WHO DO NOT DIE UP ABOVE WILL TAKE WATER EITHER HERE OR LOWER DOWN. THEY WILL GO DOWN SUCH AS LIVE, TO THE SHALLOWS OF THE SEEONEE LAIRS, AND THERE THY PACK MAY MEET THEM BY THE THROAT.
AHAI! BETTER COULD NOT BE... THERE IS NOW ONLY THE LITTLE MATTER OF THE RUN AND THE LEAP.
HAST THOU SEEN THE ROCKS ABOVE THEE? FROM THE LANDWARD SIDE?
INDEED NO. THAT I HAD FORGOT-TEN.
GO LOOK. IT IS ALL ROTTEN GROUND. ONE OF THY CLUMSY FEET SET DOWN WITH-OUT SEEING WOULD END THE HUNT. FOR THY SAKE ONLY, I WILL CARRY WORD TO THE PACK THAT THEY MAY KNOW WHERE TO LOOK FOR THE DHOLES. FOR MYSELF, I AM NOT OF ONE SKIN WITH ANY WOLF.

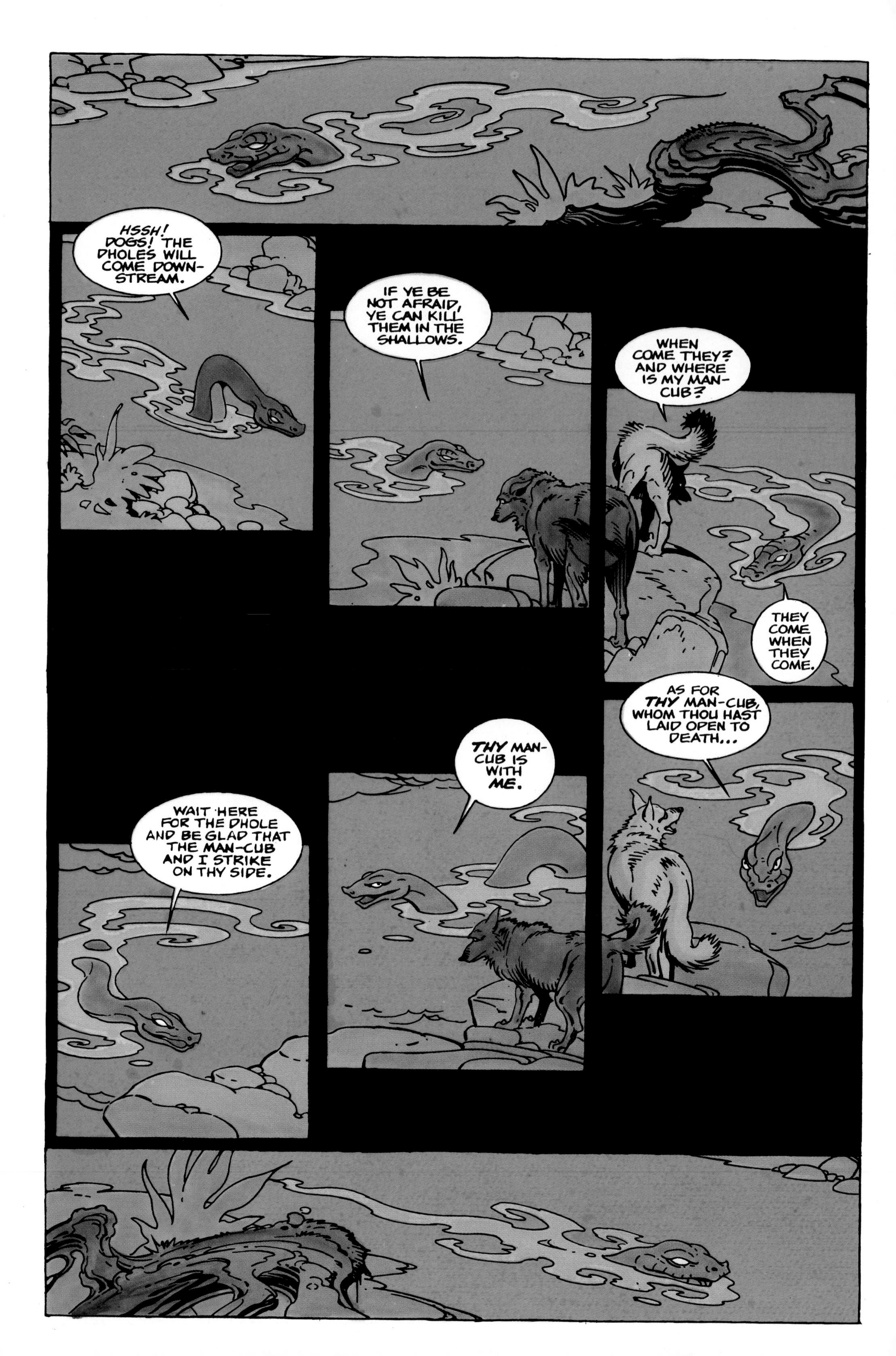
HSSH! DOGS! THE DHOLES WILL COME DOWN-STREAM.
IF YE BE NOT AFRAID, YE CAN KILL THEM IN THE SHALLOWS.
WHEN COME THEY? AND WHERE IS MY MAN-CUB?
THEY COME WHEN THEY COME.
AS FOR THY MAN-CUB, WHOM THOU HAST LAID OPEN TO DEATH...
THY MAN-CUB IS WITH ME.
WAIT HERE FOR THE DHOLE AND BE GLAD THAT THE MAN-CUB AND I STRIKE ON THY SIDE.

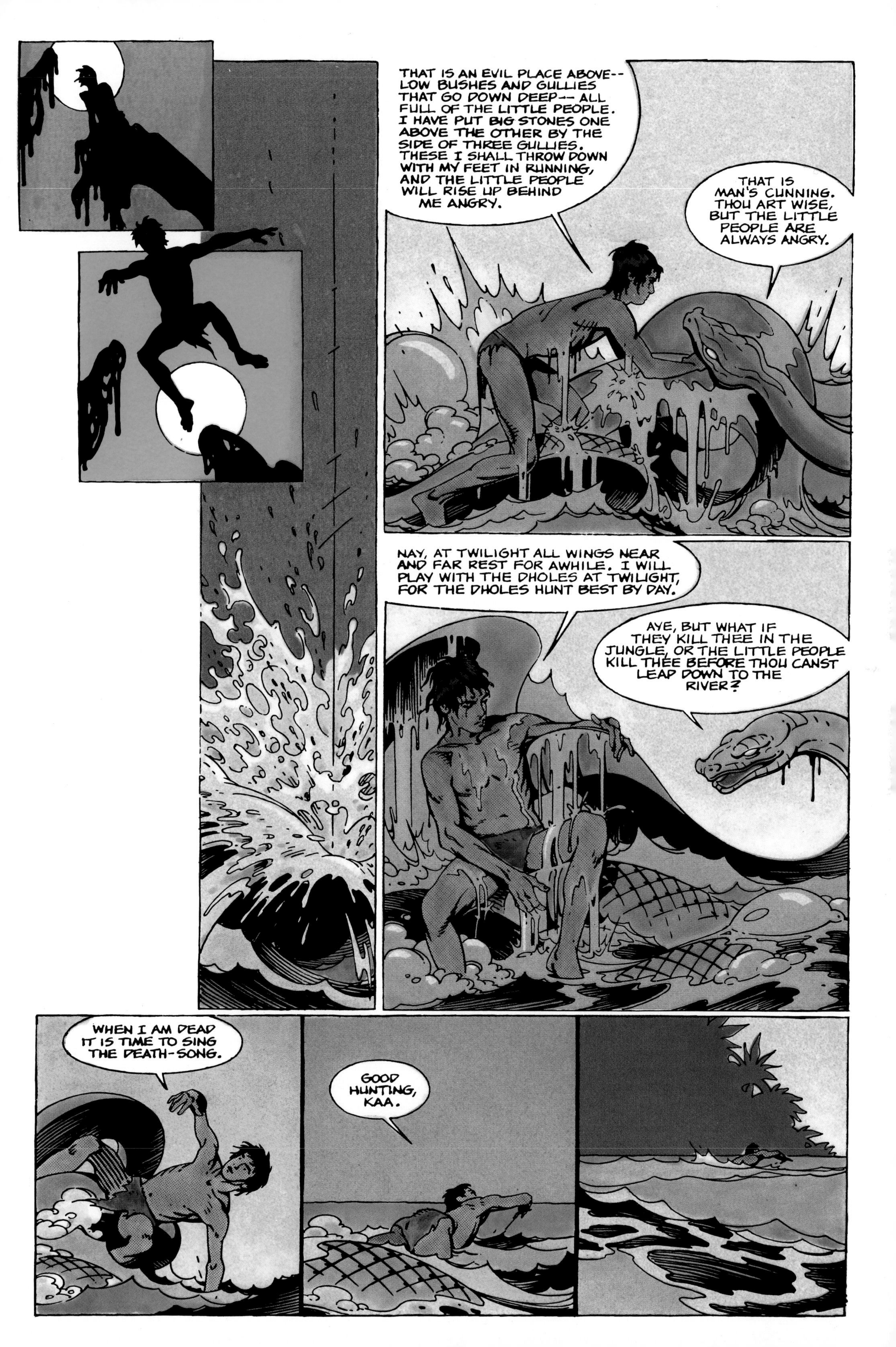
THAT IS AN EVIL PLACE ABOVE-- LOW BUSHES AND GULLIES THAT GO DOWN DEEP-- ALL FULL OF THE LITTLE PEOPLE. I HAVE PUT BIG STONES ONE ABOVE THE OTHER BY THE SIDE OF THREE GULLIES. THESE I SHALL THROW DOWN WITH MY FEET IN RUNNING, AND THE LITTLE PEOPLE WILL RISE UP BEHIND ME ANGRY.
THAT IS MAN'S CUNNING. THOU ART WISE, BUT THE LITTLE PEOPLE ARE ALWAYS ANGRY.
NAY, AT TWILIGHT ALL WINGS NEAR AND FAR REST FOR AWHILE. I WILL PLAY WITH THE DHOLES AT TWILIGHT, FOR THE DHOLES HUNT BEST BY DAY.
AYE, BUT WHAT IF THEY KILL THEE IN THE JUNGLE, OR THE LITTLE PEOPLE KILL THEE BEFORE THOU CANST LEAP DOWN TO THE RIVER?
WHEN I AM DEAD IT IS TIME TO SING THE DEATH-SONG.
GOOD HUNTING, KAA.

THERE WAS NOTHING MOWGLI LIKED BETTER THAN TO "TO PULL THE WHISKERS OF DEATH" AND MAKE THE JUNGLE FEEL THAT HE WAS THEIR OVERLORD. HE KNEW THAT THE LITTLE PEOPLE DISLIKED THE SMELL OF WILD GARLIC, SO HE GATHERED A SMALL BUNDLE OF IT AND THEN FOLLOWED WON-TOLLA'S BLOOD-TRAIL AS IT RAN SOUTHERLY FROM THE LAIRS FOR SOME FIVE MILES.

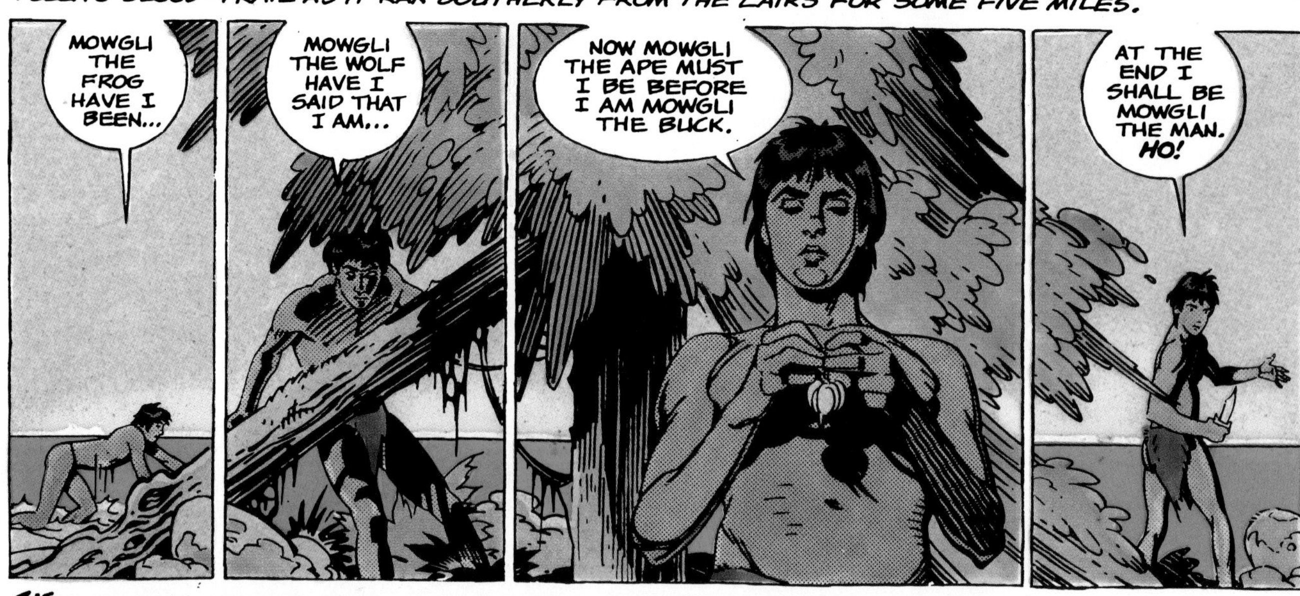

MOWGLI THE FROG HAVE I BEEN...
MOWGLI THE WOLF HAVE I SAID THAT I AM...
NOW MOWGLI THE APE MUST I BE BEFORE I AM MOWGLI THE BUCK.
AT THE END I SHALL BE MOWGLI THE MAN. HO!

WON-TOLLA'S TRAIL, ALL RANK WITH DARK BLOOD SPOTS, RAN UNDER A FOREST OF THICK TREES THAT GREW CLOSE TOGETHER AND STRETCHED AWAY NORTH-EASTWARD, GRADUALLY GROWING THINNER TO WITHIN TWO MILES OF THE BEE ROCKS. MOWGLI TROTTED ALONG UNDER THE TREES, JUDGING DISTANCES BETWEEN BRANCH AND BRANCH, TILL HE CAME TO THE OPEN GROUND, WHICH HE STUDIED VERY CAREFULLY FOR AN HOUR.

THEN HE TURNED, PICKED UP WON-TOLLA'S TRAIL WHERE HE HAD LEFT IT, AND SETTLED HIMSELF IN A TREE WITH AN OUTLYING BRANCH SOME EIGHT FEET FROM THE GROUND.

ZZZZZ
ZZZ
SNIFF SNIFF
RUFF RUFF RUFF RUFF RUFF RUFF RUFF RUFF
GOOD HUNTING! BY WHOSE LEAVE DO YE COME HERE?
RUFF RUFF RUFF
ALL JUNGLES ARE OUR JUNGLE.
DOG, RED DOG! GO BACK TO THE DEKKAN AND EAT LIZARDS. DOG, DOG, RED, RED DOG!
!
SNAP
THERE IS HAIR BETWEEN THY EVERY TOE
RRRRRRR
SNAP
SNAP
SNAP

MOWGLI LAID HIMSELF DOWN ALONG THE BRANCH, HIS RIGHT ARM FREE, AND FOR SOME FIVE MINUTES HE TOLD THE PACK WHAT HE THOUGHT AND KNEW ABOUT THEM, THEIR MANNERS, THEIR CUSTOMS, THEIR MATES, AND THEIR PUPPIES. AND SLOWLY AND DELIBERATELY HE DROVE THE DHOLES FROM SILENCE TO GROWLS, FROM GROWLS TO YELLS, AND FROM YELLS TO HOARSE SLAVERY RAVINGS.

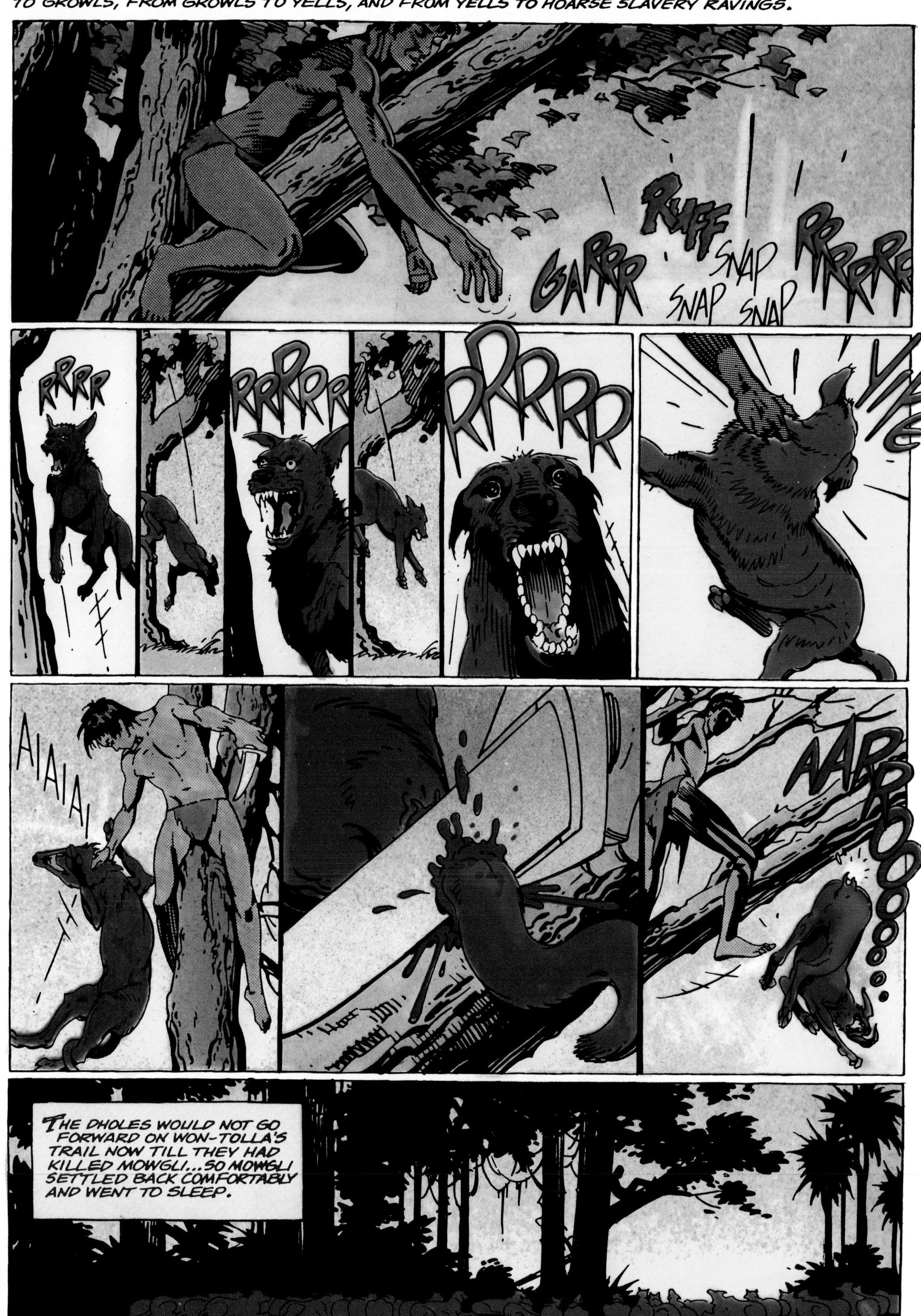
GARRR
RUFF
SNAP
SNAP
SNAP
RRRRRR
RRRR
RRRRRR
RRRRRR
YIPE
AIAIAI
AARROOOOOO
THE DHOLES WOULD NOT GO FORWARD ON WON-TOLLA'S TRAIL NOW TILL THEY HAD KILLED MOWGLI... SO MOWGLI SETTLED BACK COMFORTABLY AND WENT TO SLEEP.

SUCH FAITHFUL WATCHERS. YE BE TRUE DHOLES. BUT TO MY THINKING, TOO MUCH OF ONE KIND. FOR THAT REASON I DO NOT GIVE THE BIG LIZARD-EATER HIS TAIL AGAIN. ART THOU NOT PLEASED, RED DOG?

I MYSELF WILL TEAR OUT THY STOMACH!

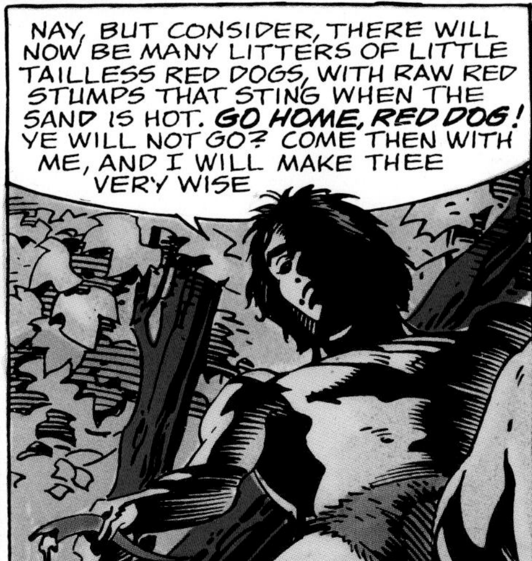

NAY, BUT CONSIDER, THERE WILL NOW BE MANY LITTERS OF LITTLE TAILLESS RED DOGS, WITH RAW RED STUMPS THAT STING WHEN THE SAND IS HOT. GO HOME, RED DOG! YE WILL NOT GO? COME THEN WITH ME, AND I WILL MAKE THEE VERY WISE

MOWGLI MOVED MONKEY-FASHION FROM TREE TO TREE, THE PACK FOLLOWING WITH LIFTED HUNGRY HEADS. NOW AND THEN HE WOULD PRETEND TO FALL, AND THE PACK WOULD TUMBLE ONE OVER THE OTHER IN THEIR HASTE TO BE IN AT THE DEATH.

WHEN HE CAME TO THE LAST TREE, HE TOOK THE GARLIC AND RUBBED HIMSELF ALL OVER CAREFULLY.

DOST THOU THINK TO COVER THY SCENT? WE WILL FOLLOW TO THE DEATH!

TAKE THY TAIL AND FOLLOW NOW....

TO THE DEATH!

RRAWRRRRRRR
RRAWWRRRRRRR
RRAWRRRRR

SKRAKK
SKRAKK
SNAP

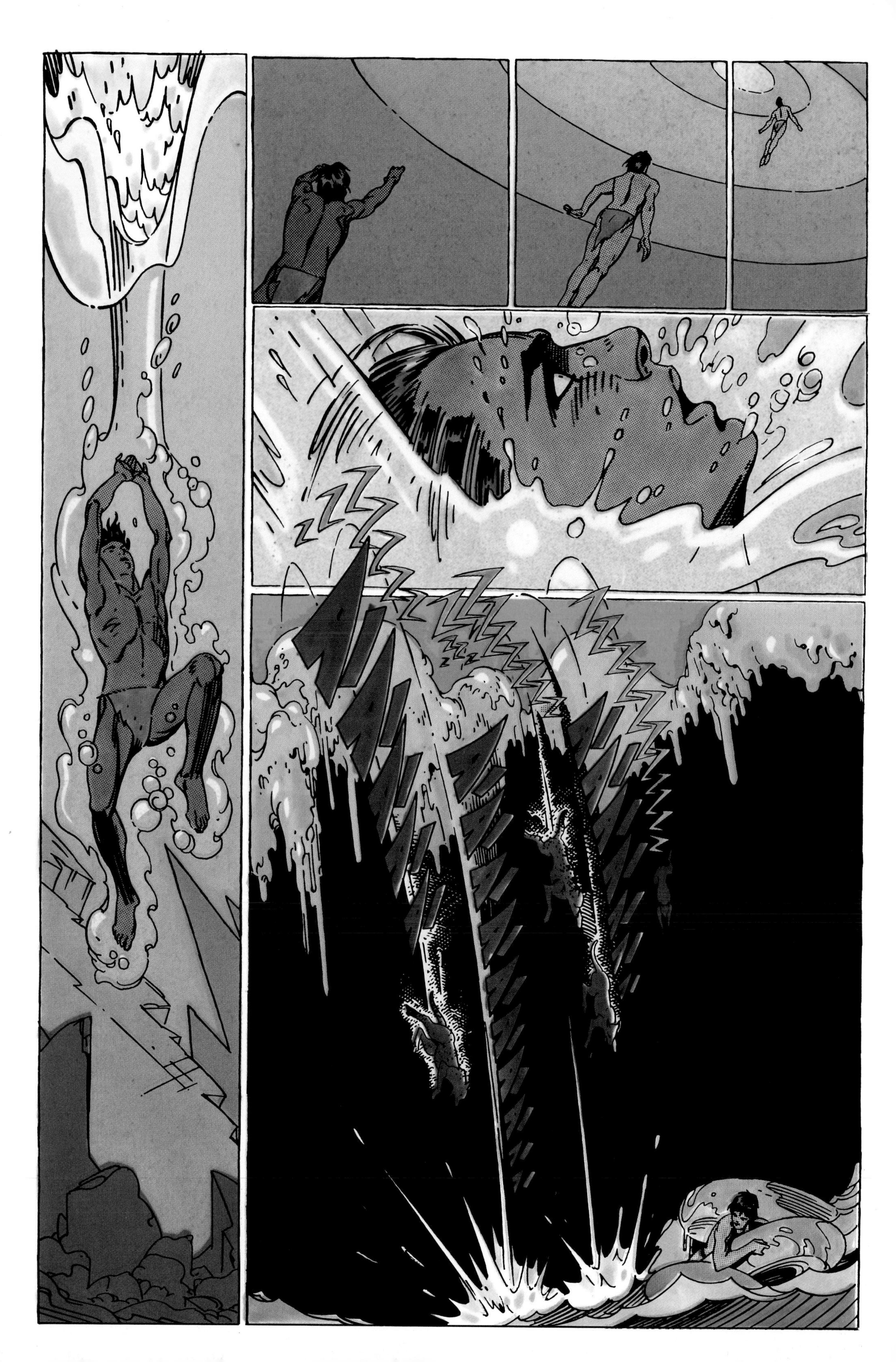

WE MAY NOT STAY HERE, THE LITTLE PEOPLE ARE ROUSED INDEED...
...AND MANY OF THE DHOLES TOOK WATER SWIFTLY WHEN THEY SAW THE LITTLE PEOPLE RISE. THEY ARE UN-HURT. COME.
THE MORE WORK FOR MY KNIFE, THEN. PHAI! HOW THE LITTLE PEOPLE FOLLOW.
THIS IS NOT GOOD HUNT-ING.
GOOD HUNTING
THUNK

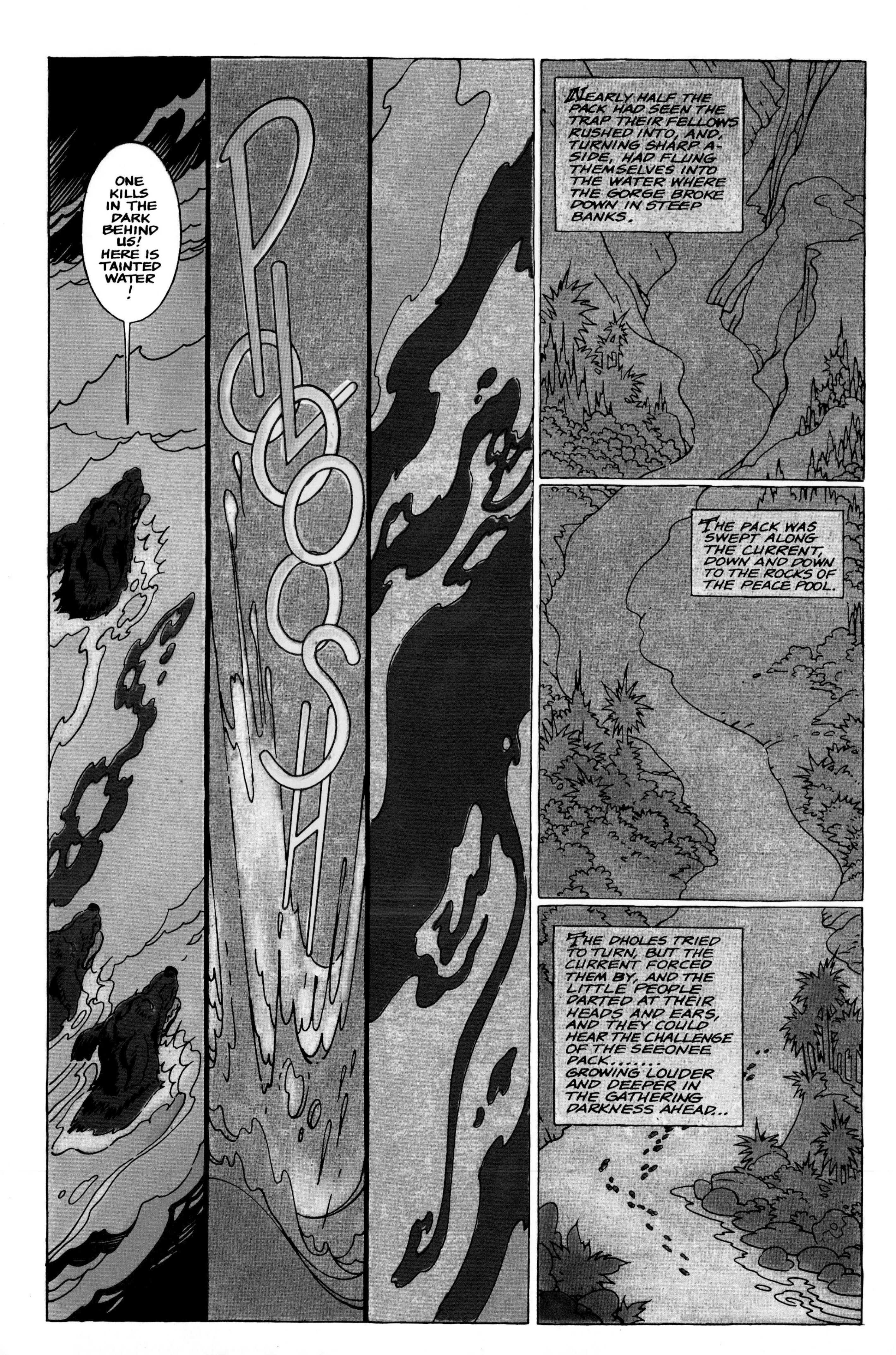
ONE KILLS IN THE DARK BEHIND US! HERE IS TAINTED WATER!
PLOOOSH
NEARLY HALF THE PACK HAD SEEN THE TRAP THEIR FELLOWS RUSHED INTO, AND, TURNING SHARP A-SIDE, HAD FLUNG THEMSELVES INTO THE WATER WHERE THE GORGE BROKE DOWN IN STEEP BANKS.
THE PACK WAS SWEPT ALONG THE CURRENT, DOWN AND DOWN TO THE ROCKS OF THE PEACE POOL.
THE DHOLES TRIED TO TURN, BUT THE CURRENT FORCED THEM BY, AND THE LITTLE PEOPLE DARTED AT THEIR HEADS AND EARS, AND THEY COULD HEAR THE CHALLENGE OF THE SEEONEE PACK.......
GROWING LOUDER AND DEEPER IN THE GATHERING DARKNESS AHEAD..

THEY COME TO THE FIGHT WITH TWO STOMACHS AND MANY VOICES. THE REST IS WITH THY BRETHREN BELOW YONDER. THE LITTLE PEOPLE GO BACK TO SLEEP, AND I WILL TURN ALSO. I DO NOT HELP WOLVES.

THEN THE LONG FIGHT BEGAN, HEAVING AND STRAINING AND SPLITTING AND SCATTERING AND NARROWING AND BROADENING ALONG THE RED WET SANDS.

A WOLF FLIES AT THE THROAT OR SNAPS AT THE FLANK, WHILE A DHOLE BITES LOW, SO WHEN THE DHOLES WERE STRUGGLING OUT OF THE WATER, THE ODDS WERE WITH THE WOLVES-- ON DRY LAND, THE WOLVES SUFFERED.

BUT IN THE WATER OR ON LAND, MOWGLI'S KNIFE CAME AND WENT THE SAME.

THE FOUR GUARDED HIS BACK AND EITHER SIDE, OR STOOD OVER HIM WHEN THE SHOCK OF A LEAPING, YELLING DHOLE WHO HAD THROWN HIMSELF ON THE STEADY BLADE BORE HIM DOWN.

FOR THE REST IT WAS ONE TANGLED CONFUSION--A LOCKED AND SWAYING MOB THAT MOVED FROM RIGHT TO LEFT AND FROM LEFT TO RIGHT ALONG THE BANK, AND ALSO GROUND ROUND AND ROUND SLOWLY ON ITS OWN CENTER.

AS THE NIGHT WORE ON, THE QUICK, GIDDY-GO-ROUND MOTION INCREASED, BUT MOWGLI FELT THAT THE END WAS COMING SOON...
THE MEAT IS VERY NEAR THE BONE!
BUT THE BONE IS YET TO BE CRACKED!
THE RED BLADE RAN LIKE A FLAME ALONG THE SIDE OF A DHOLE WHOSE HINDQUARTERS WERE HIDDEN BY THE WEIGHT OF A CLINGING WOLF.
AOWAWA! THUS DO WE IN THE JUNGLE!
MY KILL! LEAVE HIM TO ME!
WON-TOLLA, THEE! IS THY STOMACH STILL EMPTY, OUT-LIER?
BY THE BULL THAT BOUGHT ME, IT IS THE TAILLESS ONE!
IT IS NOT WISE TO KILL CUBS AND LAHINIS, UNLESS ONE ALSO KILLS THE LAIR-FATHER, AND IT IS IN MY STOMACH THAT THIS LAIR-FATHER KILLS THEE.

A DHOLE LEAPED TO HIS LEADER'S AID, BUT BEFORE HIS TEETH HAD FOUND WON-TOLLA'S FLANK, MOWGLI'S KNIFE WAS IN HIS CHEST, AND GREY BROTHER TOOK WHAT WAS LEFT.

AND THUS DO WE DO IN THE JUNGLE.

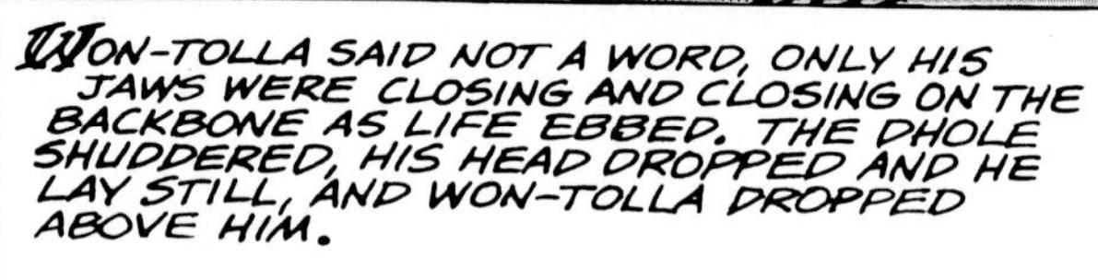

WON-TOLLA SAID NOT A WORD, ONLY HIS JAWS WERE CLOSING AND CLOSING ON THE BACKBONE AS LIFE EBBED. THE DHOLE SHUDDERED, HIS HEAD DROPPED AND HE LAY STILL, AND WON-TOLLA DROPPED ABOVE HIM.

HUH! THE BLOOD-DEBT IS PAID. SING THE SONG, WON-TOLLA.

HE HUNTS NO MORE.

THE BONE IS CRACKED! THEY GO! KILL, KILL OUT, O HUNTERS OF THE FREE PEOPLE!
THE DEBT! PAY THE DEBT! THEY HAVE SLAIN THE LONE WOLF!
LET NOT A DOG GO!
AAIIIIIIII!
AKELA!
SAID I NOT IT WOULD BE MY LAST FIGHT? IT IS GOOD HUNTING. AND THOU, LITTLE BROTHER?
I LIVE, HAVING KILLED MANY.
EVEN SO. I DIE, AND I WOULD-- I WOULD DIE BY THEE, LITTLE BROTHER.

IT IS LONG SINCE THE OLD DAYS OF SHERE KHAN AND A MAN-CUB THAT ROLLED NAKED IN THE DUST.
NAY, NAY, I AM A WOLF.
THOU ART ALL A MAN, LITTLE BROTHER, OR ELSE THE PACK HAD FLED BEFORE THE DHOLE. TODAY THOU HAST SAVED THE PACK EVEN AS I ONCE SAVED THEE. HAST THOU FORGOTTEN? ALL DEBTS ARE PAID NOW. THIS HUNTING IS ENDED. GO TO THINE OWN PEOPLE.
I WILL NEVER GO. I WILL HUNT ALONE IN THE JUNGLE.
AFTER THE RAINS COME THE SPRING. GO BACK BEFORE THOU ART DRIVEN.
WHO WILL DRIVE ME?
MOWGLI WILL DRIVE MOWGLI. GO BACK TO THY PEOPLE. GO TO MAN.
WHEN MOWGLI DRIVES MOWGLI, I WILL GO.
THERE IS NO MORE FOR THEE. NOW I WOULD SPEAK TO MY KIND. LITTLE BROTHER, CANST THOU RAISE ME TO MY FEET?
VERY CAREFULLY AND GENTLY, MOWGLI RAISED AKELA TO HIS FEET AND THE LONE WOLF DREW A DEEP BREATH AND BEGAN THE DEATH SONG. IT GATHERED STRENGTH AS HE WENT ON, LIFTING AND RINGING FAR ACROSS THE RIVER, TILL IT CAME TO THE LAST "GOOD HUNTING!"

MOWGLI SAT WITH HIS HEAD ON HIS KNEES, CARELESS OF ANYTHING ELSE, WHILE THE LAST OF THE DYING DHOLES WERE BEING OVERTAKEN AND RUN DOWN BY THE MERCILESS LAHINIS. FIFTEEN OF THE PACK, AS WELL AS HALF A DOZEN LAHINIS WERE DEAD BY THE RIVER, AND OF THE OTHERS, NOT ONE WAS UNMARKED. MOWGLI SAT THROUGH IT ALL TILL THE COLD DAY-BREAK, WHEN PHAO'S WET RED MUZZLE WAS DROPPED IN HIS HAND, AND MOWGLI DREW BACK TO SHOW THE GAUNT BODY OF AKELA.

GOOD HUNTING!

HOWL, DOGS! A WOLF HAS DIED TONIGHT.
BUT OF ALL THE PACK OF TWO HUNDRED FIGHTING DHOLES, RED DOGS OF THE DEKKAN, WHOSE BOAST IS THAT NO LIVING THING IN THE JUNGLE DARE STAND BEFORE THEM, NOT ONE RETURNED TO THE DEKKAN TO CARRY THAT NEWS.
END

PROLOGUE • TWO YEARS AFTER THE DEATH OF AKELA
MAN GOES TO MAN! CRY THE CHALLENGE THROUGH THE JUNGLE! HE THAT WAS OUR BROTHER GOES AWAY. HEAR, NOW, AND JUDGE, O YE PEOPLE OF THE JUNGLE. ANSWER, WHO SHALL TURN HIM -- WHO SHALL STAY?
MAN GOES TO MAN! HE IS WEEPING IN THE JUNGLE. HE THAT WAS OUR BROTHER SORROWS SORE! MAN GOES TO MAN! (OH, WE LOVED HIM IN THE JUNGLE!) TO THE MAN-TRAIL WHERE WE MAY NOT FOLLOW MORE.
THE YEAR TURNS, THE JUNGLE GOES FORWARD. THE TIME OF NEW TALK IS NEAR. THAT LEAF KNOWS. IT IS VERY GOOD. AOWH.
I HAD FORGOTTEN. I SHALL KNOW WHEN THE TIME OF NEW TALK IS HERE, BECAUSE THEN THOU AND THE OTHERS RUN AWAY AND LEAVE ME SINGLE-FOOT.
BUT, INDEED, LITTLE BROTHER, WE DO NOT ALWAYS-
I SAY YE DO! HOW WAS IT LAST SEASON WHEN I WOULD GATHER SUGAR-CANE FROM THE FIELDS OF A MAN PACK? I SENT A RUNNER -- I SENT THEE! -- TO HATHI BIDDING HIM TO COME AND PLUCK THE SWEET GRASS FOR ME WITH HIS TRUNK. HE DID NOT COME UPON THE NIGHT WHEN I SENT HIM THE WORD. I SAW HIM TRUMPETING IN THE MOONLIGHT, YET HE WOULD NOT COME.
AND I AM THE MASTER OF THE JUNGLE.
IT WAS THE TIME OF NEW TALK. PERHAPS, LITTLE BROTHER, THOU DIDST NOT THAT TIME CALL HIM BY A MASTER WORD?
I DO NOT KNOW -- NOR DO I CARE. LET US SLEEP, BAGHEERA. MY STOMACH IS HEAVY IN ME.
IN AN INDIAN JUNGLE THE SEASONS SLIDE ONE INTO THE OTHER ALMOST WITHOUT DIVISION. THERE IS ONE DAY WHEN ALL THINGS FEEL OLD AND USED. THEN THERE IS ANOTHER DAY -- TO THE EYE NOTHING WHATEVER HAS CHANGED -- WHEN ALL THE SMELLS ARE NEW AND DELIGHTFUL AND THE WHISKERS OF THE JUNGLE-PEOPLE QUIVER TO THEIR ROOTS... UP TO THIS YEAR MOWGLI HAD ALWAYS DELIGHTED IN THE TURN OF THE SEASONS. BUT THAT SPRING, AS HE TOLD BAGHEERA, HIS STOMACH WAS NEW IN HIM...

The Spring Running by Rudyard Kipling
THE MORNING CAME THAT THE SMELLS HAD CHANGED AND MOR THE PEACOCK CRIED IT ALOUD ALL ALONG THE MISTY WOODS...
BUT WHEN MOWGLI OPENED HIS MOUTH TO SEND ON THE CRY, THE WORDS CHOKED BETWEEN HIS TEETH, AND A FEELING CAME OVER HIM THAT BEGAN AT HIS TOES AND ENDED IN HIS HAIR-- A FEELING OF PURE UNHAPPINESS.
THE SMELLS HAVE CHANGED. GOOD HUNTING, LITTLE BROTHER! WHERE IS THY ANSWER?
LITTLE BROTHER
GOOD HUNTING
WHERE IS THY ANSWER?
GOOD HUNTING
LITTLE BROTHER
WHERE IS THY ANSWER?
ANSWER
GOOD HUNTING
ANSWER
WHERE IS THY ANSWER?
ADAPTED FOR COMICS BY P. CRAIG RUSSELL — OP. 40.

A LIGHT SPRING RAIN — ELEPHANT RAIN THEY CALL IT — DROVE ACROSS THE JUNGLE IN A BELT HALF-A-MILE WIDE, LEFT THE NEW LEAVES WET AND NODDING BEHIND, AND DIED OUT IN A DOUBLE RAINBOW AND A LIGHT ROLL OF THUNDER.

THE SPRING-HUM BROKE OUT AND ALL THE JUNGLE-FOLK SEEMED TO BE GIVING TONGUE AT ONCE. ALL EXCEPT MOWGLI.
I HAVE EATEN GOOD FOOD. I HAVE DRUNK GOOD WATER. BUT MY STOMACH IS HEAVY AND I HAVE, FOR NO GOOD CAUSE, GIVEN VERY BAD TALK TO BAGHEERA AND OTHERS. NOW, TOO, I AM HOT AND NOW I AM COLD, AND NOW I AM NEITHER HOT NOR COLD, BUT ANGRY WITH THAT WHICH I CANNOT SEE.
HUHH! IT IS TIME TO MAKE A RUNNING! TO THE MARSHES OF THE NORTH AND BACK AGAIN. THE FOUR SHALL COME WITH ME, FOR THEY GROW AS FAT AS WHITE GRUBS.

HE CALLED, BUT NEVER ONE OF THE FOUR ANSWERED. THEY WERE FAR BEYOND EARSHOT, SINGING OVER THE SPRING SONGS.

YES, LET THE RED DHOLE COME FROM THE DEKKAN OR THE RED FLOWER DANCE AMONG THE BAMBOOS, AND ALL THE JUNGLE RUNS WHINING TO MOWGLI, CALLING HIM GREAT ELEPHANT NAMES.

BUT NOW, BECAUSE EYE-OF-THE-SPRING IS RED, AND MOR MUST SHOW HIS NAKED LEGS IN SOME SPRING DANCE, THE JUNGLE GOES MAD AS TABAQUI...

BY THE BULL THAT BOUGHT ME, AM I THE MASTER OF THE JUNGLE, OR AM I NOT?

WHAT?

IT WAS A COUPLE OF YOUNG WOLVES LOOKING FOR OPEN GROUND ON WHICH TO FIGHT THAT DASHED MOWGLI ASIDE TO THE EARTH. HE WAS ON HIS FEET ALMOST BEFORE HE FELL. HIS WHITE TEETH WERE BARED AND AT THAT MINUTE HE WOULD HAVE KILLED THEM BOTH FOR NO OTHER REASON BUT THAT THEY WERE FIGHTING WHEN HE WISHED THEM TO BE QUIET.

HE DANCED AROUND THEM WITH LOWERED SHOULDERS AND QUIVERING HAND, READY TO SEND A DOUBLE BLOW WHEN THE FIRST FLURRY OF THE SCUFFLE SHOULD BE OVER. BUT WHILE HE WAITED, THE STRENGTH SEEMED TO BE OUT OF HIS BODY.

?!

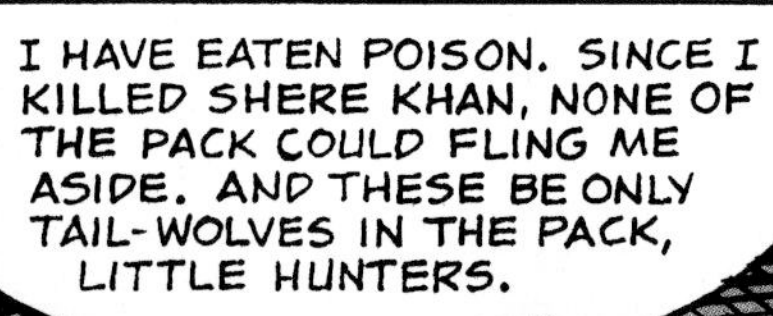
I HAVE EATEN POISON. SINCE I KILLED SHERE KHAN, NONE OF THE PACK COULD FLING ME ASIDE. AND THESE BE ONLY TAIL-WOLVES IN THE PACK, LITTLE HUNTERS.

MY STRENGTH IS GONE FROM ME, AND PRESENTLY I SHALL DIE. O, MOWGLI, WHY DOST THOU NOT KILL THEM BOTH ?

MOWGLI WAS LEFT ALONE ON THE TORN AND BLOODY GROUND, LOOKING NOW AT HIS KNIFE, AND NOW AT HIS LEGS AND ARMS, WHILE THE FEELING OF UNHAPPINESS HE HAD NEVER KNOWN BEFORE COVERED HIM AS WATER COVERS A LOG.
HE KILLED EARLY THAT EVENING AND ATE BUT LITTLE, SO AS TO BE IN GOOD FETTLE FOR HIS SPRING RUNNING, AND HE ATE ALONE BECAUSE ALL THE JUNGLE-PEOPLE WERE AWAY SINGING OR FIGHTING.

IT WAS A PERFECT WHITE NIGHT, AS THEY CALL IT. ALL GREEN THINGS SEEMED TO HAVE MADE A MONTH'S GROWTH SINCE THE MORNING. THE BRANCH THAT WAS YELLOW-LEAVED THE DAY BEFORE DRIPPED SAP WHEN MOWGLI BROKE IT. THE MOSSES CURLED DEEP AND WARM OVER HIS FEET, THE YOUNG GRASS HAD NO CUTTING EDGES, AND ALL THE VOICES OF THE JUNGLE BOOMED LIKE ONE DEEP HARP-STRING TOUCHED BY THE MOON-- THE FULL MOON OF NEW TALK.

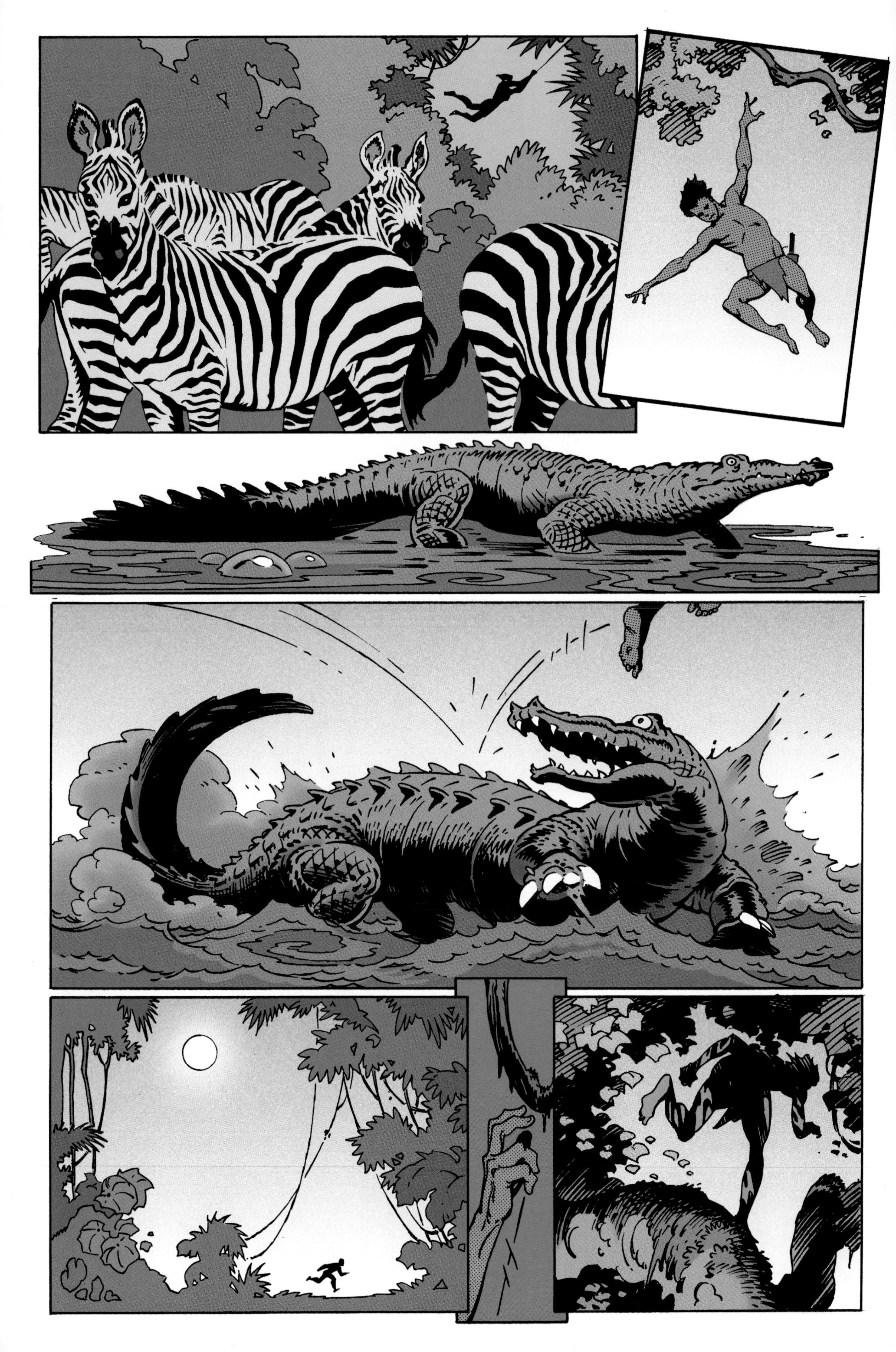

SO HE RAN, SOMETIMES SHOUTING, SOMETIMES SINGING TO HIMSELF. THE HAPPIEST THING IN ALL THE JUNGLE THAT NIGHT TILL THE SMELL OF THE FLOWERS WARNED HIM THAT HE WAS NEAR THE MARSHES, AND THOSE LAY FAR BEYOND HIS FARTHEST HUNTING GROUND.

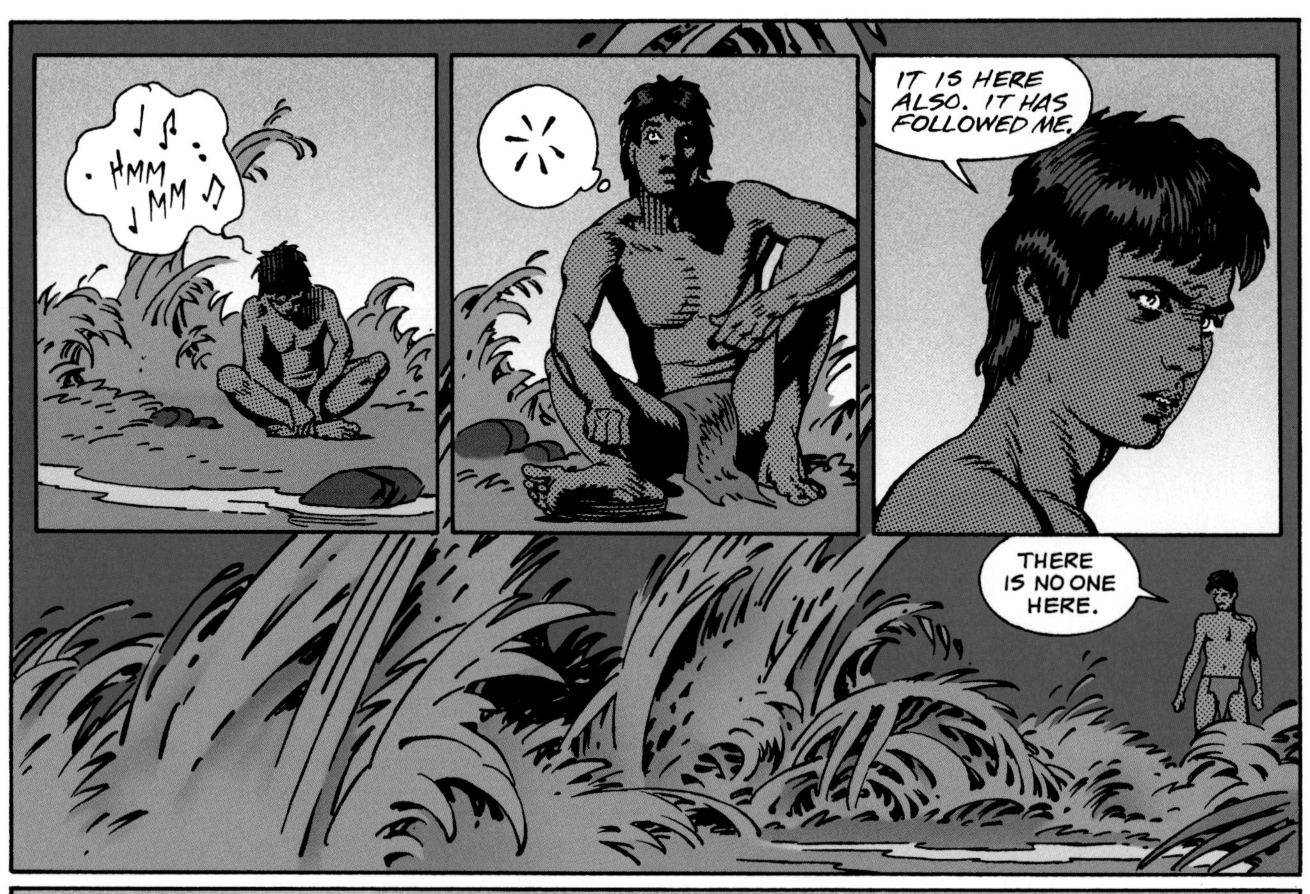

HMM
MM
IT IS HERE ALSO. IT HAS FOLLOWED ME.
THERE IS NO ONE HERE.

CAW CAW CAW CAW CA

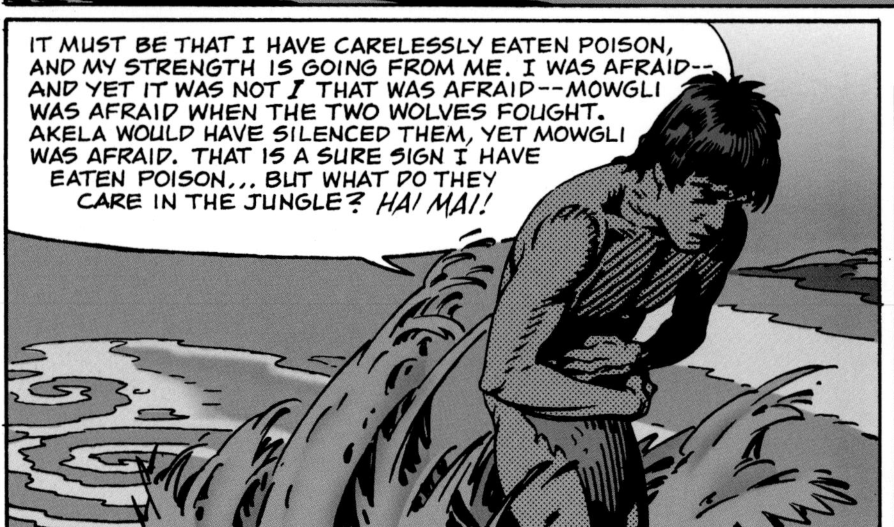

IT MUST BE THAT I HAVE CARELESSLY EATEN POISON, AND MY STRENGTH IS GOING FROM ME. I WAS AFRAID-- AND YET IT WAS NOT *I* THAT WAS AFRAID--MOWGLI WAS AFRAID WHEN THE TWO WOLVES FOUGHT. AKELA WOULD HAVE SILENCED THEM, YET MOWGLI WAS AFRAID. THAT IS A SURE SIGN I HAVE EATEN POISON... BUT WHAT DO THEY CARE IN THE JUNGLE? *HAI MAI!*

HE WAS SO SORRY FOR HIMSELF THAT HE NEARLY WEPT.

AND AFTER, THEY WILL FIND ME LYING IN THE BLACK WATER.

A LARGE WARM TEAR SPLASHED DOWN ON HIS KNEE, AND, MISERABLE AS HE WAS, MOWGLI FELT HAPPY THAT HE WAS SO MISERABLE, IF YOU CAN UNDERSTAND THAT UPSIDE-DOWN SORT OF HAPPINESS.

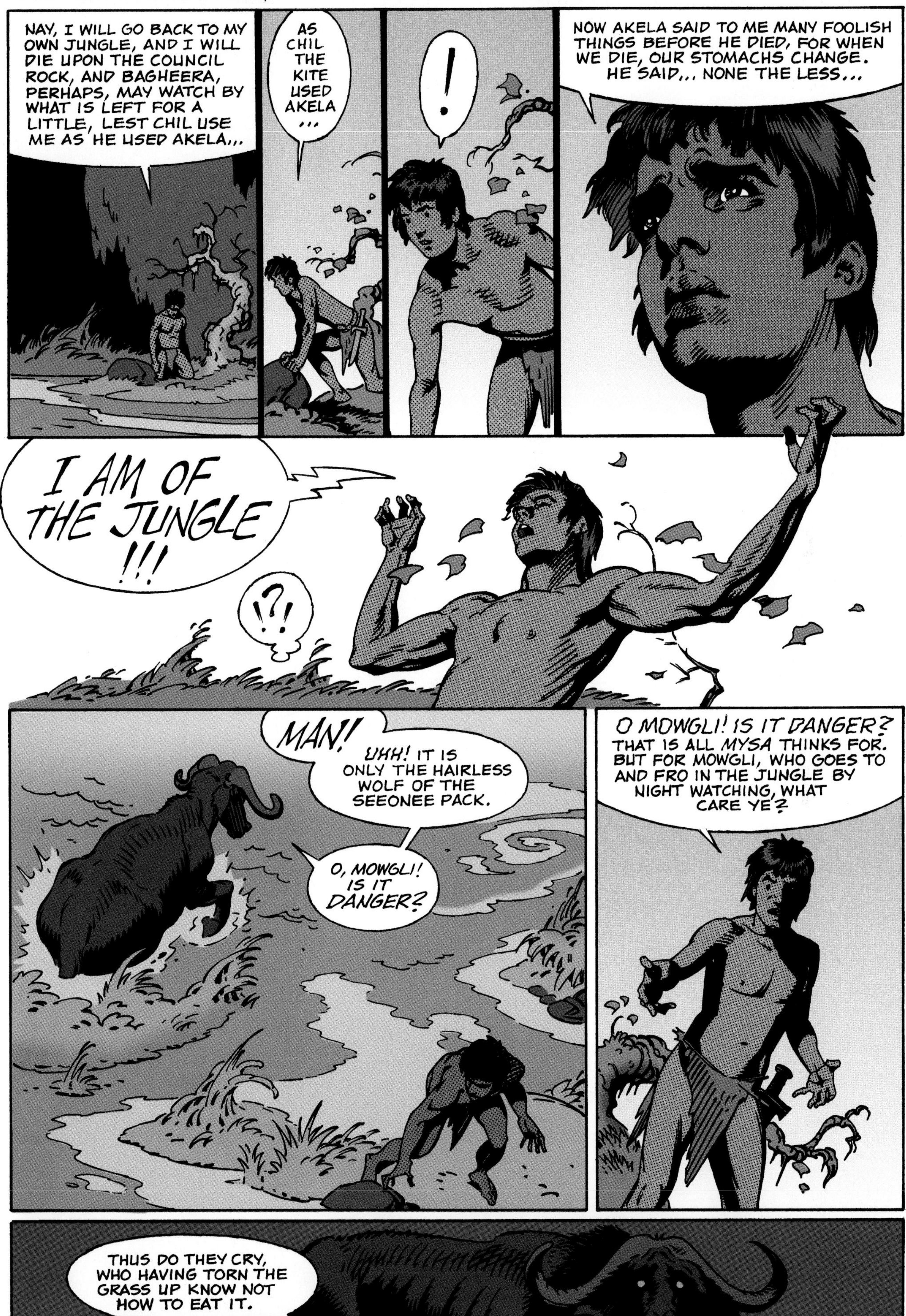

HMMPH! I WILL NOT DIE HERE! MYSA, WHO IS ONE BLOOD WITH JACALA AND THE PIG, WOULD MOCK ME. NEVER HAVE I RUN SUCH A SPRING RUNNING-- HOT AND COLD TOGETHER. UP, MOWGLI!

MAROOOOOO
WEEEEEHAHAHA
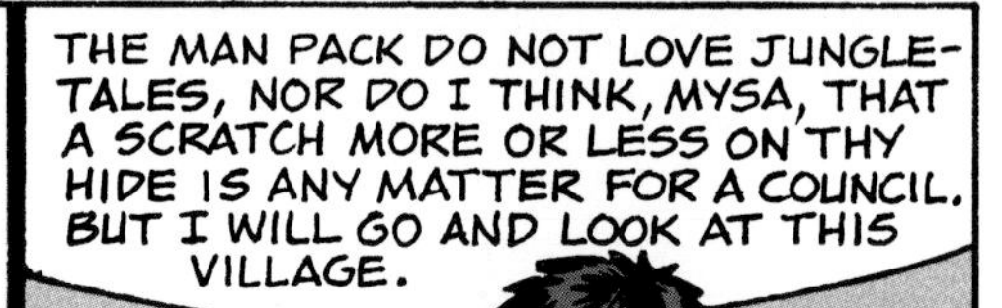
WOLF! THOU? WHAT HUNTER WOULD HAVE CRAWLED LIKE A SNAKE AMONG THE LEECHES FOR A MUDDY JEST-A JACKEL'S JEST. -- SUCH A MAN'S BRAT AS SHOUTS IN THE DUST BY THE CROPS YONDER...
WHAT MAN PACK LAIR HERE BY THE MARSHES, MYSA? THIS IS NEW JUNGLE TO ME.
GO NORTH, THEN. IT WAS A NAKED COW-HERD'S JEST. GO AND TELL THEM AT THE VILLAGE AT THE FOOT OF THE MARSH.
THE MAN PACK DO NOT LOVE JUNGLE-TALES, NOR DO I THINK, MYSA, THAT A SCRATCH MORE OR LESS ON THY HIDE IS ANY MATTER FOR A COUNCIL. BUT I WILL GO AND LOOK AT THIS VILLAGE.
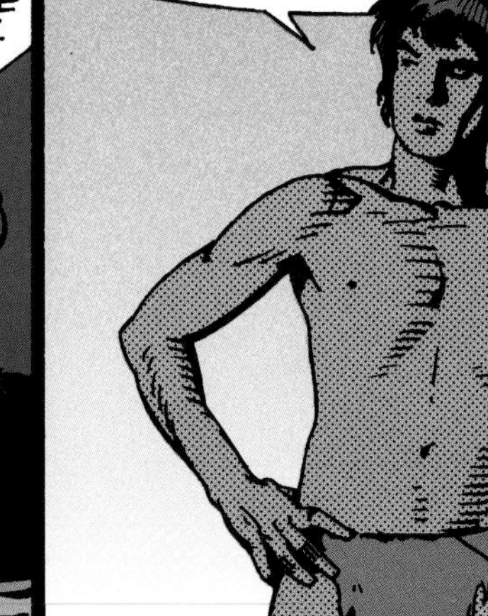

SOFTLY NOW! IT IS NOT EVERY NIGHT THAT THE MASTER OF THE JUNGLE COMES TO HERD THEE.

THE MARSH ENDED IN A BROAD PLAIN WHERE A LIGHT TWINKLED. IT WAS A LONG TIME SINCE MOWGLI HAD CONCERNED HIMSELF WITH THE DOINGS OF MEN, BUT THIS NIGHT THE GLIMMER OF THE RED FLOWER DREW HIM FORWARD AS IF IT HAD BEEN NEW GAME.

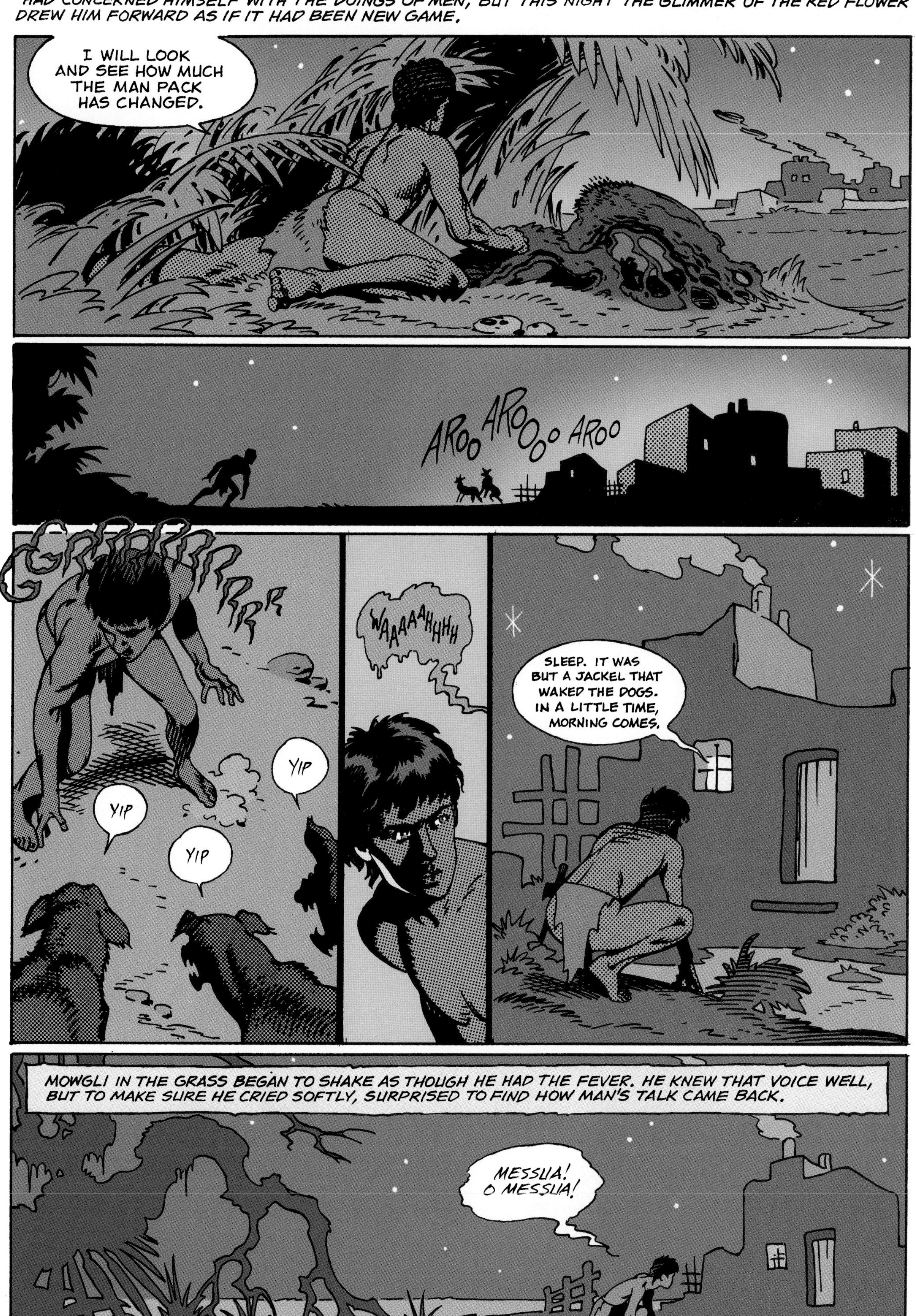

WHO CALLS?
HAST THOU FORGOTTEN?
IF IT BE THOU, WHAT NAME DID I GIVE THEE? SAY!
NATHOO! OHE' NATHOO!
COME! MY SON!
COME
MY SON...
BUT IT IS NO LONGER MY SON. IT IS A GODLING OF THE WOODS.
AHAI!
WAAHHHH
WHAT WILT THOU EAT OR DRINK? THIS IS ALL THINE. WE OWE OUR LIVES TO THEE.
BUT ART THOU HIM I CALLED NATHOO, OR A GODLING, INDEED?
I AM NATHOO. I AM VERY FAR FROM MY OWN PLACE. I SAW THIS LIGHT AND CAME HITHER. I DID NOT KNOW THOU WAST HERE.

AFTER WE CAME TO THE KHANHI-WARA THE ENGLISH WOULD HAVE HELPED US AGAINST THOSE VIL-LAGERS THAT SOUGHT TO BURN US OUT. REMEMBEREST THOU?
INDEED I HAVE NOT FOR-GOTTEN.
BUT WHEN THE ENGLISH LAW WAS MADE READY, WE WENT TO THE VILLAGE OF THOSE EVIL PEOPLE AND IT WAS NO MORE TO BE FOUND.
THAT ALSO I RE-MEMBER.
MY MAN THEREFORE TOOK SERVICE IN THE FIELDS, AND AT LAST WE HELD A LITTLE LAND HERE.
WHERE IS HE-- THE MAN THAT DUG IN THE DIRT WHEN HE WAS AFRAID ON THAT NIGHT?
HE IS DEAD-- A YEAR.
AND HE?
MY SON THAT WAS BORN TWO RAINS AGO. AND IF THOU ART NATHOO WHOM THE TIGERS CARRIED AWAY, HE IS THY YOUNGER BRO-THER. GIVE HIM AN ELDER BROTHER'S BLESSING.
HAI MAI!
WHAT DO I KNOW OF THE THING CALLED A BLESSING?

O MOTHER, MOTHER, MY HEART IS HEAVY IN ME.

I WILL MAKE A FIRE AND THOU SHALT DRINK WARM MILK.

MOWGLI SAT DOWN. ALL MANNER OF STRANGE FEELINGS WERE RUNNING OVER HIM, EXACTLY AS THOUGH HE HAD BEEN POISONED, AND HE FELT DIZZY AND A LITTLE SICK.

SON, HAVE ANY TOLD THEE THAT THOU ART BEAUTIFUL BEYOND ALL MEN?
HAH?
I AM THE FIRST THEN? THOU ART VERY BEAUTIFUL. NEVER HAVE I LOOKED UPON SUCH A MAN.
?
HA HA
NAY, THOU MUST NOT MOCK THY BROTHER. WHEN THOU ARE ONE-HALF AS FAIR, WE WILL MARRY THEE TO THE DAUGHTER OF A KING AND THOU SHALT RIDE GREAT ELEPHANTS.

MOWGLI COULD NOT UNDERSTAND ONE WORD IN THREE OF THE TALK HERE; THE WARM MILK WAS TAKING EFFECT ON HIM AFTER HIS FORTY MILE RUN; SO HE CURLED UP AND IN A MINUTE WAS DEEP ASLEEP, FOR HIS INSTINCTS, WHICH NEVER WHOLLY SLEPT, WARNED HIM THERE WAS NOTHING TO FEAR.

AHH HUNH AHH HUNH

THERE WERE ONLY A FEW COARSE CAKES BAKED OVER THE SMOKY FIRE, SOME RICE, AND A LUMP OF SOUR PRESERVED TAMARINDS -- JUST ENOUGH TO GO ON WITH TILL HE COULD GET TO HIS EVENING KILL. THE SMELL OF THE DEW IN THE MARSHES MADE HIM HUNGRY AND RESTLESS. HE WANTED TO FINISH HIS SPRING RUNNING, BUT THE CHILD INSISTED ON SITTING IN HIS ARMS, AND MESSUA WOULD HAVE IT THAT HIS LONG BLUE-BLACK HAIR MUST BE COMBED OUT.
IF THOU ART A GODLING, GIVE THY LITTLE BROTHER THE FAVOUR OF THE JUNGLE THAT HE MAY BE SAFE AMONG THY PEOPLE AS WE WERE SAFE ON THAT NIGHT IN THE JUNGLE.
HAI. I AM NEIGHER A GODLING NOR HIS BROTHER SO HOW CAN I...
AAAAEEEEEE
SNUFFLE SNK
DO NOT BRING THY-THY SERVANTS WITH THEE.
WE HAVE ALWAYS LIVED AT PEACE WITH THE JUNGLE.
OUT AND WAIT. YE WOULD NOT COME WHEN I CALLED.
IT IS PEACE. THINK OF THAT NIGHT ON THE ROAD TO KHANHI-WARA. THERE WERE SCORES OF SUCH FOLK BEFORE THEE AND BEHIND THEE. BUT I SEE THAT EVEN IN SPRING-TIME THE JUNGLE-PEOPLE DO NOT ALWAYS FORGET. MOTHER, I GO.
GRRRR

COME BACK! SON OR NO SON, COME BACK AGAIN, FOR I LOVE THEE.
BY NIGHT OR DAY THIS DOOR IS NEVER SHUT TO THEE.
I WILL SURELY COME BACK.
AND NOW, I HAVE A LITTLE CRY AGAINST THEE, GREY BROTHER. WHY CAME YE NOT, ALL FOUR, WHEN I CALLED SO LONG AGO?
SO LONG AGO? IT WAS BUT LAST NIGHT. I-WE-WERE SINGING IN THE JUNGLE, THE NEW SONGS, FOR THIS IS THE TIME OF NEW TALK. AND AS SOON AS THE SONGS WERE SUNG, I FOLLOWED THY TRAIL.. BUT, O LITTLE BROTHER, WHAT HAST THOU DONE - EATING AND SLEEPING WITH THE MAN PACK?
IF YE HAD COME WHEN I CALLED, THIS HAD NEVER BEEN.
AND NOW WHAT IS TO BE?

LOOK.
AHH
AAAIIEEE
NICE.

THE BLACK ONE SPOKE TRUTH.
"MAN GOES TO MAN AT THE LAST."
WHAT DOST THOU SAY, GREY BROTHER?
THEY CAST THEE OUT ONCE, WITH BAD TALK. THEY CUT THY MOUTH WITH STONES. THEY SENT BULDEO TO SLAY THEE. THEY WOULD HAVE THROWN THEE INTO THE RED FLOWER. THOU, NOT NOT I, HAST SAID THAT THEY ARE EVIL AND SENSELESS. THOU, AND NOT I -- I FOLLOW MY OWN PEOPLE -- DIDST LET IN THE JUNGLE UPON THEM. THOU AND NOT I DIDST MAKE SONG AGAINST THEM MORE BITTER EVEN THAN OUR SONG AGAINST RED DOG.

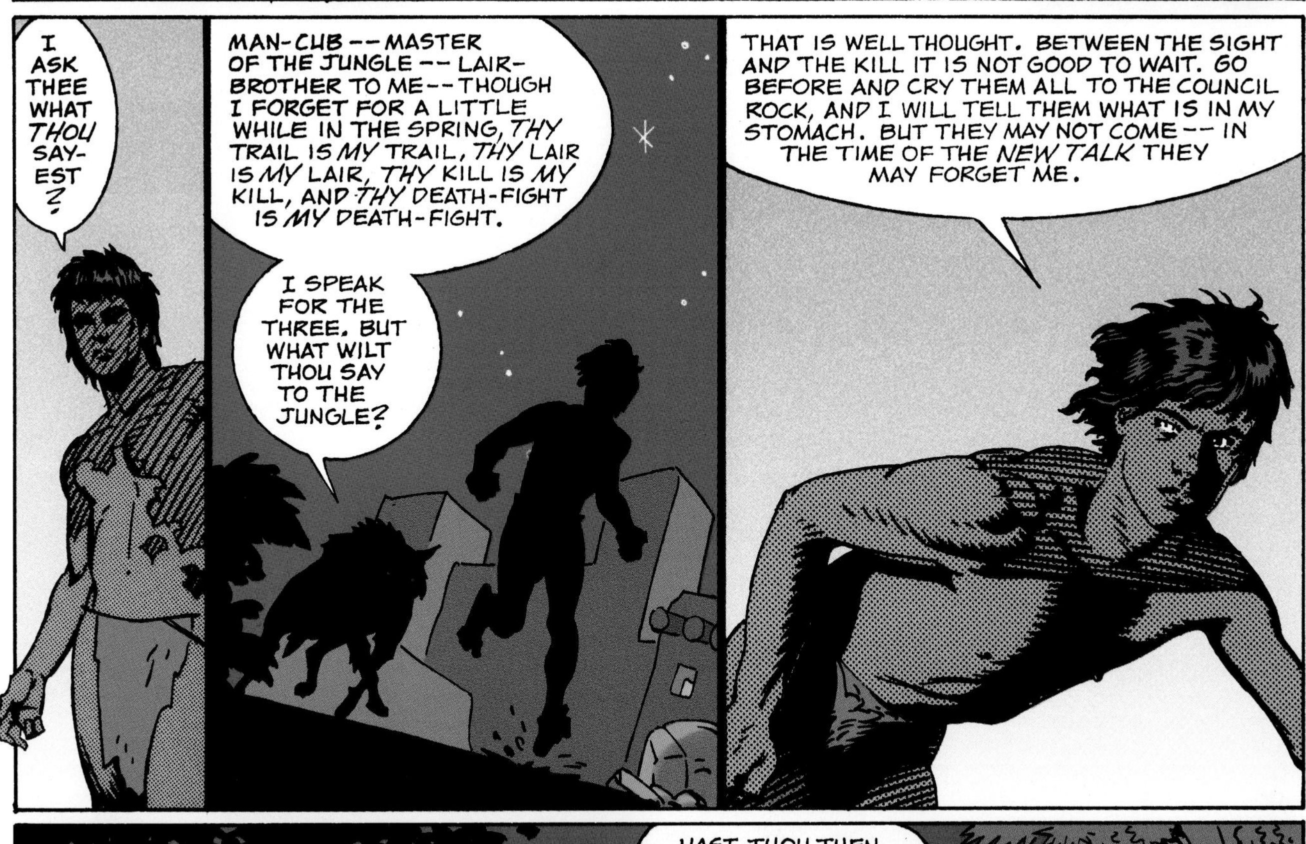
I ASK THEE WHAT *THOU* SAYEST?
MAN-CUB -- MASTER OF THE JUNGLE -- LAIR-BROTHER TO ME -- THOUGH I FORGET FOR A LITTLE WHILE IN THE SPRING, *THY* TRAIL IS *MY* TRAIL, *THY* LAIR IS *MY* LAIR, *THY* KILL IS *MY* KILL, AND *THY* DEATH-FIGHT IS *MY* DEATH-FIGHT.
I SPEAK FOR THE THREE. BUT WHAT WILT THOU SAY TO THE JUNGLE?
THAT IS WELL THOUGHT. BETWEEN THE SIGHT AND THE KILL IT IS NOT GOOD TO WAIT. GO BEFORE AND CRY THEM ALL TO THE COUNCIL ROCK, AND I WILL TELL THEM WHAT IS IN MY STOMACH. BUT THEY MAY NOT COME -- IN THE TIME OF THE *NEW TALK* THEY MAY FORGET ME.

HAST THOU THEN FORGOTTEN NOTHING?

AT ANY OTHER SEASON HIS NEWS WOULD HAVE CALLED ALL THE JUNGLE TOGETHER WITH BRISTLING NECKS, BUT NOW THEY WERE BUSY HUNTING AND FIGHTING AND KILLING AND SINGING.

THE MASTER OF THE JUNGLE GOES BACK TO MAN. COME TO THE COUNCIL ROCK.
HE WILL RETURN IN THE SUMMER HEATS.
THE RAINS WILL DRIVE HIM TO THE LAIR
RUN AND SING WITH US, GREY BROTHER.

BUT THE MASTER OF THE JUNGLE GOES BACK TO MAN.

EEE YOWA? IS THE TIME OF NEW TALK ANY LESS GOOD FOR THAT?

THE TRAIL ENDS HERE, THEN, MANLING?

WHY WAS I NOT TORN IN TWO BY RED DOG? MY STRENGTH IS GONE FROM ME, AND IT IS NOT THE POISON.
I CALL AND NONE CRY AGAIN, BUT IT IS AS THOUGH ONE LISTENED AND KEPT BACK THE ANSWER. I LIE DOWN, BUT I DO NOT REST. I RUN THE SPRING RUNNING, BUT I AM NOT MADE STILL. I BATHE, BUT I AM NOT MADE COOL. THE KILL SICKENS ME, BUT I HAVE NO HEART TO FIGHT EXCEPT I KILL. THE RED FLOWER IS IN MY BODY, MY BONES ARE WATER--AND--I KNOW NOT WHAT I KNOW.
WHAT NEED OF TALK? AKELA BY THE RIVER SAID IT, THAT MOWGLI SHOULD DRIVE MOWGLI BACK TO THE MAN PACK. I SAID IT. BUT WHO LISTENS NOW TO BALOO?
BAGHEERA--WHERE IS BAGHEERA THIS NIGHT? HE KNOWS ALSO. IT IS THE LAW.
I TAUGHT THEE THE LAW AND THOUGH I CANNOT NOW SEE THE ROCKS BEFORE ME, I SEE FAR. I SAW THEE PLAYING YONDER WHEN THOU WAST A LITTLE FROG: AND BAGHEERA, THAT BOUGHT THEE FOR THE PRICE OF A YOUNG BULL NEWLY KILLED, SAW THEE ALSO.
OF THAT LOOKING-OVER, WE TWO ONLY REMAIN, FOR RAKSHA, THY LAIR-MOTHER IS DEAD WITH THY LAIR-FATHER; THE OLD WOLF PACK IS LONG SINCE DEAD; THOU KNOWEST WHERE SHERE KHAN WENT, AND AKELA DIED AMONG THE DHOLES, WHERE BUT FOR THY WISDOM AND STRENGTH, THE SECOND SEEONEE PACK WOULD ALSO HAVE DIED. THERE REMAIN NOTHING BUT OLD BONES.
LITTLE FROG, TAKE THINE OWN TRAIL; MAKE THY LAIR WITH THINE OWN BLOOD AND PACK AND PEOPLE; BUT WHEN THERE IS NEED OF FOOT OR TOOTH OR EYE OR A WORD CARRIED SWIFTLY BY NIGHT, REMEMBER, MASTER OF THE JUNGLE, THE JUNGLE IS THINE AT CALL.

HAI MAI, MY BROTHERS, I KNOW NOT WHAT I KNOW. I WOULD NOT GO, BUT I AM DRAWN BY BOTH FEET. HOW SHALL I LEAVE THESE NIGHTS?
NAY, LITTLE BROTHER, THERE IS NO SHAME IN THIS HUNTING. WHEN THE HONEY IS EATEN WE LEAVE THE EMPTY HIVE.
HAVING CAST THE SKIN, WE MAY NOT CREEP INTO IT AFRESH. IT IS THE LAW.
LISTEN, DEAREST OF ALL TO ME. THERE IS NEITHER WORD NOR WILL HERE TO HOLD THEE BACK.
LOOK UP!
WHO MAY QUESTION THE MASTER OF THE JUNGLE?
IT IS NO LONGER THE MAN-CUB THAT ASKS LEAVE OF HIS PACK, BUT THE MASTER OF THE JUNGLE THAT CHANGES HIS TRAIL.
WHO SHALL QUESTION MAN IN HIS WAYS?
BUT BAGHEERA AND THE BULL THAT BOUGHT ME-- I WOULD NOT--
RRRRAAARRRRR

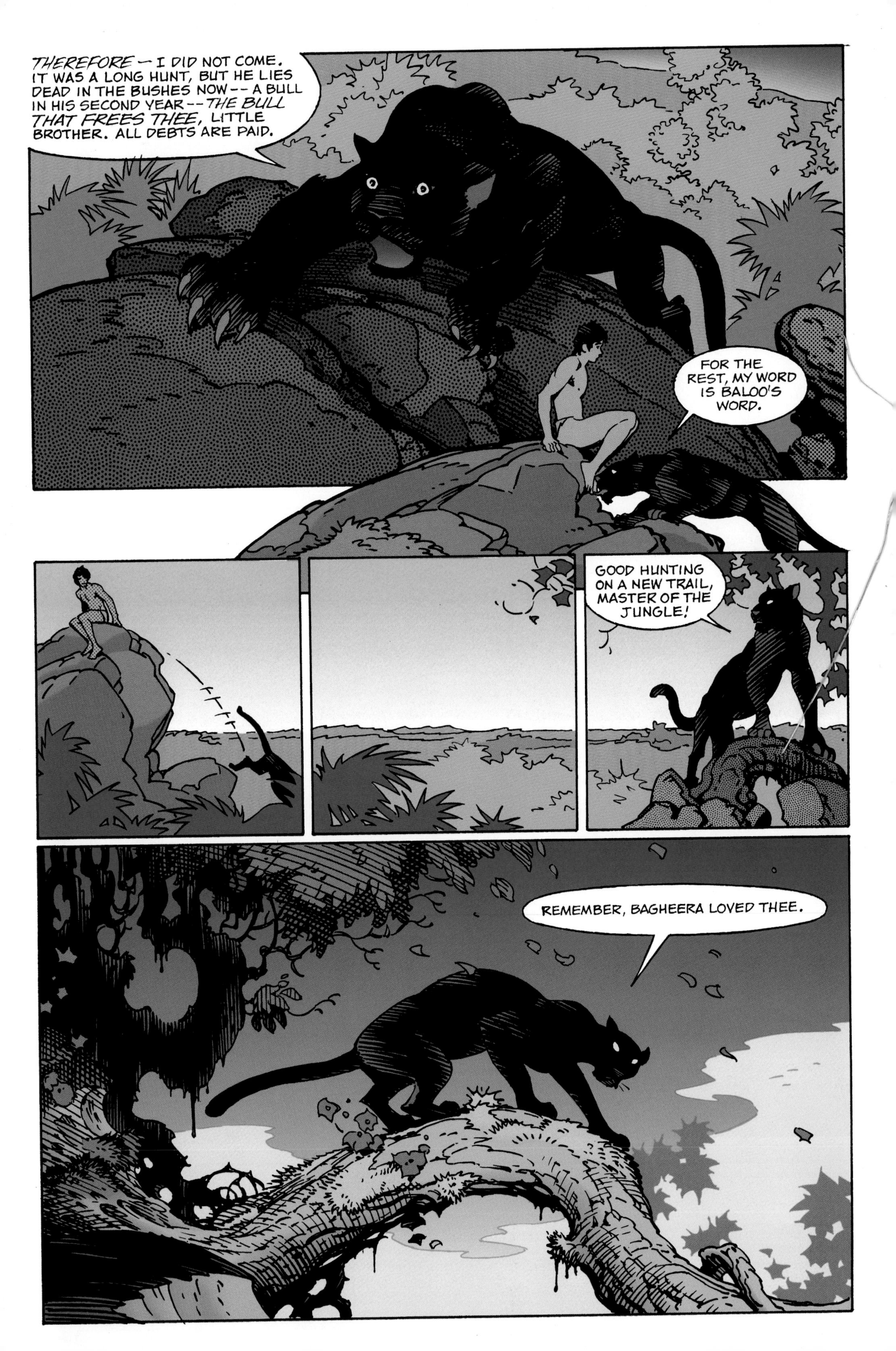
THEREFORE — I DID NOT COME. IT WAS A LONG HUNT, BUT HE LIES DEAD IN THE BUSHES NOW -- A BULL IN HIS SECOND YEAR -- THE BULL THAT FREES THEE, LITTLE BROTHER. ALL DEBTS ARE PAID.
FOR THE REST, MY WORD IS BALOO'S WORD.
GOOD HUNTING ON A NEW TRAIL, MASTER OF THE JUNGLE!
REMEMBER, BAGHEERA LOVED THEE.

THOU HAST HEARD. THERE IS NO MORE. GO NOW, BUT FIRST COME TO ME...

O WISE LITTLE FROG, COME TO ME!

IT IS HARD TO CAST THE SKIN.

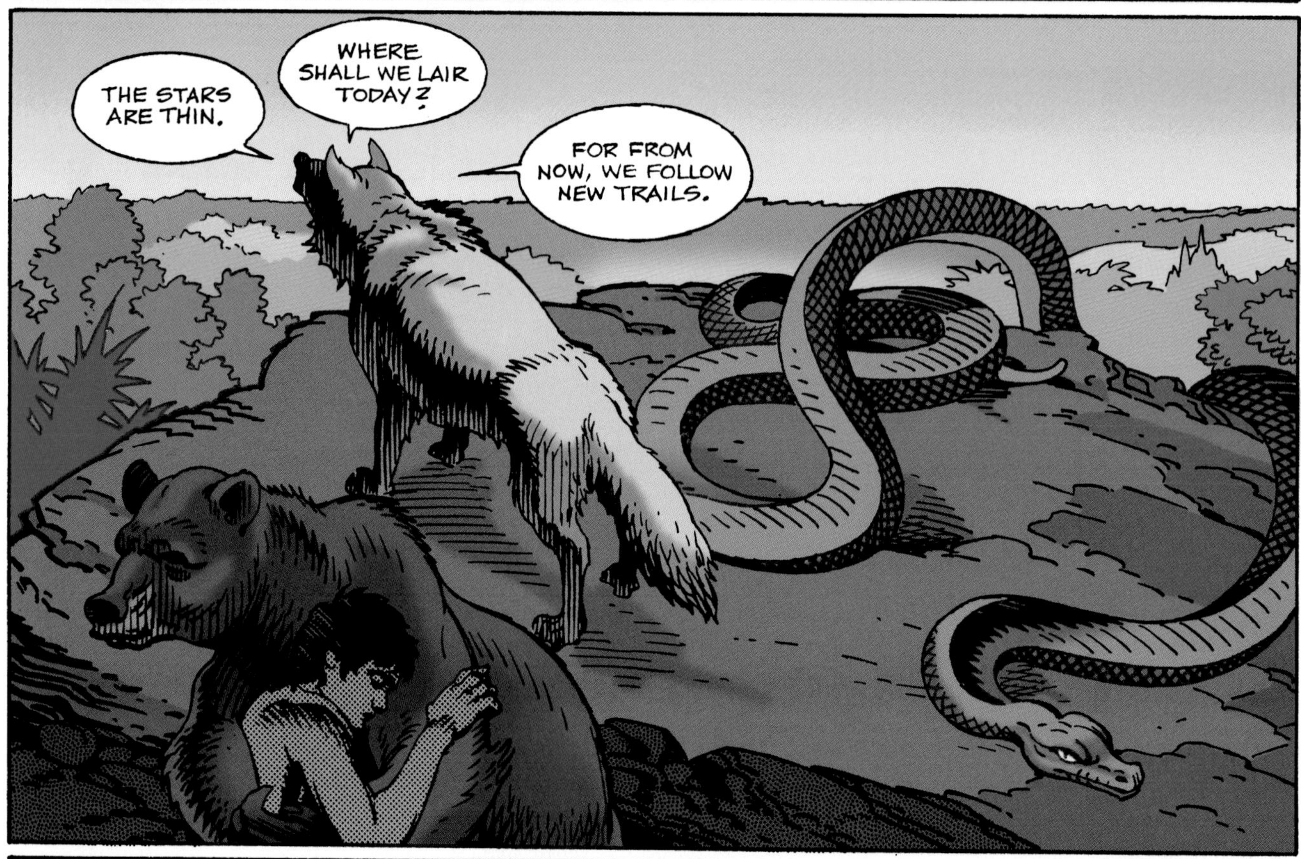
THE STARS ARE THIN.
WHERE SHALL WE LAIR TODAY?
FOR FROM NOW, WE FOLLOW NEW TRAILS.

AND THIS IS THE LAST OF THE MOWGLI STORIES.

EPILOGUE
The
·OUTSONG·
THIS IS THE SONG THAT MOWGLI HEARD BEHIND HIM
IN THE JUNGLE TILL HE CAME TO MESSUA'S DOOR AGAIN
"ON THE TRAIL THAT THOU MUST TREAD
TO THE THRESHOLD OF OUR DREAD
WHERE THE FLOWER BLOSSOMS RED;
THROUGH THE NIGHTS WHEN THOU SHALT LIE
PRISONED FROM OUR MOTHER SKY
HEARING US, THY LOVES GO BY;
IN THE DAWNS WHEN THOU SHALT WAKE
TO THE TOIL THOU CANST NOT BREAK,
HEARTSICK FOR THE JUNGLE'S SAKE;
WOOD AND WATER, WIND AND TREE
JUNGLE FAVOUR GO WITH THEE."
END